# REVERENCE IN THE WILDERNESS

## FRONTIER HEARTS
### BOOK THREE

## ANDREA BYRD

Copyright © 2024 by Andrea Byrd

All rights reserved. No portion of this book may be reproduced or transmitted in any form or by any means - photocopied, shared electronically, scanned, stored in a retrieval system, or other - without the express permission of the publisher. Exceptions will be made for brief quotations used in critical reviews or articles promoting this work.

The characters and events in this fictional work are the product of the author's imagination. Any resemblance to actual people, living or dead, is coincidental.

Unless otherwise indicated, all Scripture quotations are taken from the Holy Bible, Kings James Version.

ISBN-13: 978-1-942265-85-6

*For all the women who have ever experienced a miscarriage or threatened miscarriage.*

# CHAPTER 1

*May 14, 1782—Green County, Kentucky*

Keturah Elliot's heart seized as the vicious waters swallowed her mother whole.

"Ma!" Her brother Duncan's deep voice echoed in her ears before he ran past her, his dark hair a blur as he dove into the churning river.

*Nay!* Her mind screamed the word, but her tongue remained as frozen as the rest of her body. Her feet were glued to the rocky bank beneath her as she stood, helpless, as her only sibling was consumed as well. Tears slipped down her cheeks as she watched and waited. But neither her mother nor her brother ever emerged again.

A hand at her elbow pulled Keturah from the

memory. She blinked past her tears to focus on the fresh mound of dirt that marked her father's grave. She swallowed the lump in her throat as his words from that day came back to her. *'Tis all yer fault. We ne'er shoulda crossed.*

After unclenching her jaw, Keturah turned and offered her only friend in the world the barest of smiles. "Thank ye for comin'." Her voice rasped more than she would have liked it to as she included Margaret's husband, Iain, in her nod. Their home was a day and a half's journey from hers on foot, but when she had shown up at their door, they immediately leapt to her aid. If it were not for Iain, she did not know how she would have pulled her father's body from the battered barn or buried him. Dugan Elliot had been an exceedingly large man, as broad as he was tall.

"Ma." A quiet little voice drew Keturah's attention to the dark-headed toddler nestled within Margaret's petticoats. "Me play?" His bright blue eyes petitioned his mother along with his words, drawing a grin from both women.

Iain spoke up. "Why dinnae we go hunt up Miss Blair some more wood for her wood pile?"

"Aye." The boy's face lit up, and he quickly abandoned his post for his father's outstretched hand.

Margaret shot a grateful glance at her husband before she wrapped an arm around Keturah's shoulders and urged her toward the large double-pen cabin that stood at the edge of the meadow. Much like the now-caved-in barn beside it, it was far too sizeable for only her and her father. But the man had been bent on building up the grandest homestead in Kentucky. Instead, a tornado had claimed both him and the barn.

Keturah frowned at the mangled remnants of the building before Margaret ushered her inside. *Lord, what am I to do now?*

In the mere four days since her father's passing, Keturah had run over scenario after scenario in her mind. Yet she balked at the one solution that kept coming to mind.

While Keturah settled on the bench beside the long dining table, Margaret hung a kettle and stoked the fire in the massive stone fireplace. The fireplace was built of stones that she and her father had collected from the countless nearby streams. It had taken ages to acquire enough for the massive structure, but she had to admit, it had been well worth the effort. Her mother would have loved the natural beauty of the hearth.

"We will have tea directly," Margaret informed her with a gentle smile as she came to settle across from Keturah.

"What am I goin' to do?" The words tumbled out of her before she had a chance to stop them. While she did not wish to appear weak, there was no denying that her situation was precarious.

Margaret's mouth pressed into a line. "I have seen

3

firsthand how dangerous it can be for a woman alone in this wilderness, an' I think ye should come an' stay with me an' Iain."

Keturah's gaze jerked to the other woman's face. "Nay. I cannae lose this farm." Her heart kicked up a notch, pounding in her chest.

Though she and her father rarely saw eye to eye, they had put too much time and energy into settling the land for her to walk away. Nay, she could not fail. With no one left to help her father, he had counted on her labor in addition to expecting all the normal women's chores to be completed. The land around them had been watered with her blood, sweat, and tears multiple times over, and she would not see it gone in a single storm. Tension coiled in her shoulders.

Margaret's hand covered hers. "I know how hard it would be to leave, but I believe it to be for the best." When Keturah looked up, compassion and concern shone in her friend's eyes. Margaret had her best interests at heart—of that, she was sure. And she spoke from experience, having been the victim of a brutal attack that sent her away from her own home to the safety of a fort for some time. But there had to be another way.

Sensing her hesitation, Margaret amended her statement. "If ye will not leave, we will come an' help ye as we can."

Keturah nodded but closed her eyes, praying for some option she had yet to consider. Again, a nagging voice within her offered up the same solution she had tamped down countless times. But this time, it seemed to echo within her mind, refusing to be pushed away. She glanced heavenward, where a dark ceiling greeted her. This could not be the Lord's will.

Yet the urging did not waver. Keturah heaved a sigh and released the words that had been rolling around in her mind. "I have to take a husband."

Across from her, Margaret sucked in a breath. "Yer sure?"

Nay, she was not. Unease swirled in her stomach at the thought. What if the man turned out to be as callous and controlling as her father? But, to keep the land, the home she and her father had built with their own hands, it seemed to be the only viable solution. Surely, she could find someone she could tolerate working alongside. She forced her chin to dip in confirmation.

"Do ye have someone in mind?"

Keturah's shoulders sagged. "Nay. But James Skaggs's Station is barely a day's travel from here, an' I suspect there should be some single men around there."

Margaret's eyes widened before she seemed to think through her answer. She gave a nod before she stood and picked up a towel. After moving over to the hearth, she lifted the kettle from its hook and brought it over to prepare their tea. She stood at the end of the table, hands braced against the sturdy wood as steam wafted from the two cups in front of her, swirling upward in front of her deep-orange dress. "The Lord can bless a marriage of convenience. After all, me an' Iain are livin' proof of that. As yer friend, though, it concerns me, ye marryin' a man ye dinnae know. Me an' Iain would be more than willin' to travel with ye to the station."

Keturah shook her head. "Nay. I have to do this on me own. I traveled to get ye an' Iain on me own before, an' this is not near as far. All will be well." Was she trying to convince Margaret or herself?

Her friend came around the table and clasped a reassuring hand on her arm as she placed a cup of tea before her. "Then we will pray. Pray that God provides ye with a good, lovin' husband. A man of faith."

Margaret slid onto the seat next to her and began the prayer. Keturah listened intently but could not seem to commit her heart to the words. If she had to take a husband, it ought to be a man she could come to love and cherish as Margaret did her husband. However, especially under the circumstances, that seemed too much to ask.

She breathed in a deep breath and let out a shaky sigh. *Lord, please just dinnae let me lose the farm.* She would gladly settle for a marriage of mere contentment if only she could make the farm a success.

*D*aniel sat astride the beautiful chestnut mare he had purchased for his trip west as he surveyed the green waters of Big Brush Creek. It was to be their last water crossing before reaching James Skaggs's Station, which was situated near one of the creek's tributaries. It appeared much more the breadth and depth of a river, rather than a simple creek, though. A muscle rippled in his mare's shoulder, causing him to grip the reins tighter.

While Cinnamon was stunning and sure-footed, the man who had sold her to Daniel had neglected to explain that she was also skittish and high strung. Not exactly the greatest fit for an inexperienced rider whose confidence in his horsemanship skills was still lacking after more than a month of travel. Back east, his family had always had the use of a carriage and driver, so he had never had a reason to gain experience. And unlike his five brothers, he had never taken a personal interest in the activity. While he did hold an affinity for animals, he was more likely to be found in the stables talking to the horses rather than out riding them.

A clatter of rocks drew Daniel's attention from his musings to the family that had approached the water's edge to his right. Worry lines stretched across the middle-aged mother's forehead as she watched the first men crossing. Her husband gripped her shoulder tightly while three small children gathered around them. The youngest, a toddler with white-blond hair matching that of his parents, crept closer to the water, a hand outstretched. But the woman took hold of his shoulder before his fingertips could reach the liquid. Daniel glanced about. With no horse near and their bodies laden with packs and supplies, it appeared that they were traveling on foot like so many of the impoverished families in their travel party.

"One of the children can ride across with me," Daniel offered. Though the waters appeared relatively still, he had quickly learned during their crossings that creeks such as this still held a dangerous current that could sweep away an inexperienced swimmer. Like a child.

The mother looked at her husband, who nodded. He stepped forward and lifted the toddler into Daniel's arms. "Take Charlie here, if you do not mind. He has not yet learned to swim."

"Of course, I would be glad to." Daniel smiled down at the man. "He will be quite safe up here on Cinnamon with me." As Daniel accepted the boy and settled him in front of him in the saddle, the man nodded. But his gaze lingered on his son as though he was not quite convinced.

Still, as it was his turn to cross, Daniel held tightly to the boy and asked Cinnamon to step forward into the creek. The mare had taken only two steps when she dislodged a large flat rock with the edge of her hoof. Her weight flipped the stone upward with a loud splash before it smacked against the side of her hock.

Cinnamon went reeling backward, her head high in the air and nostrils flaring. The black stallion behind her lashed out as she encroached upon his space, nipping her flank with his teeth.

Daniel's heart rate kicked up a notch as the mare surged forward and spun away from the other horse. Suddenly, his perch in the saddle seemed quite precarious. As Cinnamon plunged into the creek, water and muddy debris sprayed all around. Daniel jerked on the reins. In protest of his rough handling, she reared. Time seemed to freeze as her brown mane flew up into Daniel's face and he slipped from the saddle. Frantic, he gripped young Charlie tight to his chest and allowed the reins to slip through his hands. His body slammed into the rock-strewn bank just before Cinnamon's weight crashed atop him and the boy. Blinding pain seared through the back of his skull.

"Char..." The child's name started as a hoarse whisper before it died on his lips, black spots claiming his vision.

~

Daniel gripped the smooth edge of the rocking chair's arm as his foot bounced against the hardwood floor beneath. Guilt and worry gnawed his insides in turns. Fire crackled in the Skaggs's fireplace a few feet away. And though it had worked to dry his wet breeches at first, the warmth had grown stifling as he waited for word on Charlie's condition. If it were not for Mary Skaggs's watchful eye as she prepared the evening meal and the fact that dizziness claimed him if he attempted to stand, he would be pacing the room. Still, he chanced a glance in the middle-aged woman's direction.

As though she felt his gaze, Mrs. Skaggs lifted her eyes from the potatoes she was peeling and raised her dark brows as if to inquire if he needed assistance. Daniel forced a tight-lipped smile and lifted his hand to acknowledge all was well. But all was not well.

Upon their arrival at the station, Daniel had been whisked inside so that the stationmaster's wife could tend to the gash on the back of his head. Meanwhile, Charlie had been taken to the nearby home of the acting physician. If any lasting harm came to the boy due to his incompetence...

His chest tightened, and the pounding in his head intensified. Daniel closed his eyes against the pain.

They snapped open a moment later when the cabin door scraped across the floor. Martin Brown, the leader of their expedition, stepped in from the gathering dusk. His mouth was pulled into a grim line as he approached, causing Daniel to sit up straighter.

"Is the boy well?"

"Yes, he is well." Mr. Brown did not elaborate, his gaze on the crackling fire as he sat down on the low stone hearth beside him.

Daniel's pulse picked up as he stared down at the

man. What was the man not telling him? And why did he avoid his gaze?

When Martin finally looked him in his face, his blue gaze held a heavy dose of regret. Daniel's heart plummeted. "The boy suffered a broken arm. It will mend, though, and he is resting now. Children are resilient."

All the breath left Daniel's lungs as he sagged back against the rocker. A chill swept through his body. He opened his mouth to apologize, but Mr. Brown held up a hand to stop him, asking his own question instead. "How is your head?"

Daniel attempted to focus despite his racing thoughts. Did his head even hurt anymore? He gingerly placed a hand near where Mrs. Skaggs had stitched him up. "Um, nothing too terrible." Not when there was a child suffering.

"Good." The other man nodded and took a deep breath. "Even so, 'twill be best for you to stay here and recuperate for a few days. For your horse as well."

Daniel's gaze jerked up. "What happened to Cinnamon?"

Mr. Brown's countenance relaxed slightly. Evidently, the topic of the horse was an easier subject. "Only a strain to the left hind. She will be well in a couple of days. But everyone else will be leaving in the morning to push farther west."

Daniel's heart plummeted. "Without me."

Another thin-mouthed nod from the man before

him. "This will be a good place for you to settle. Here, near the station."

Where Daniel would be safe, looked after. Where there would be people to help him because he was not capable of succeeding on his own. Though Mr. Brown tried to make the situation sound appealing, Daniel knew what he really meant. He had failed too many times and was a hindrance to the group. No longer was he allowed to travel with them. Daniel pushed a smile onto his face despite the lifelong wound that was opening inside his chest. "Yes. You are quite right. This will be a wonderful place to settle. A beautiful land, indeed."

Mr. Brown stood and clasped him on the shoulder. "I am glad you are able to see it that way." Then he strode from the cabin, leaving Daniel to accept his fate alone.

For the millionth time, it seemed, he had been cast aside, unwanted. Just as when his father had hired a nanny to tend to his raising so that he would not have to face the child that had taken his wife from him. When his father had restricted his brothers from consorting with him or purposefully left him behind during family outings. And finally, when his father had pressed money into his hand on his eighteenth birthday and revealed that he had secured Daniel passage west to make a name for himself. Not a tear was shed upon his departure. In fact, no one besides Nanny had bid him farewell.

It was a dream twisted into a nightmare. Daniel had planned to approach his father regarding funding for furthering his education. Though it was foolish, he had spent his life dreaming of becoming a professor. Within the walls of books was the only place he felt at home. Well, his father had given him money—not enough for further education, but enough to start a modest life with. But what was he to do with it?

# CHAPTER 2

*MAY 15, 1782*

"Do not worry, boy. I know what it is to be a failure," the dark-haired man seated along the creek bank lamented to the animal beside him as he ruffled its light-brown ears. "But that does not mean you do not deserve a home and love. If nothing else, you can make a person smile." As the small creature jumped up on his knee, pink tongue lolling, the man's mouth pulled into a grin. But the gesture did not reach his eyes, and his shoulders remained slumped as he rubbed where the brown fur turned to black across the animal's back.

Something inside Keturah's chest clenched, and guilt washed over her that she had been spying. It had been inadvertent, though, with her happening upon the scene as she neared Skaggs's Station.

As she stepped out from behind the trees which had concealed her approach, Keturah purposefully sent a stone skittering across the rocky bank with the toe of her low-heeled boot. Warm sunshine kissed her cheeks as she sloshed through the shallow creek to where the stranger scrambled to his feet.

"Oh. Hello. I did not realize anyone was there." He brushed his hands against the front of his black waistcoat.

Was that silk? The cream-colored kerchief at his throat certainly was. Keturah could not recall the last time she had laid eyes on such fanciful clothing. Before they had come west, to be sure.

When the man extended his hand to her in welcome, Keturah slipped hers into his. And though his hand was softer than she would have expected, warmth spread up her arm as his strong grip easily engulfed hers. Her lips parted as her eyes flew up to his. His warm, golden gaze met hers as he grinned down at her, his chin well above the top of her head.

Keturah quickly withdrew her hand and cleared her throat. "I am sorry. I didna mean to surprise ye."

The man's smile broadened. "A most pleasant surprise, I am sure. If you do not mind me asking, are you Irish?"

"Scottish," Keturah corrected. "Me parents immigrated soon after they were married."

The man gave her a little bow. "Well, it is very nice to meet you, Mrs...?"

"Miss Keturah Elliot." Pride at both her heritage and the Christian name given by her mother swelled in her chest. This man was like no one she had ever met before. Such genteel manners for a chance meeting in the woods. "An' ye are...?"

"Daniel. Daniel Scott."

A yapping sound brought their attention downward, to the white, brown, and black foxhound pup that twirled in a circle before jumping up to settle his front paws against her petticoats.

A low chuckle emanated from the man before her. "And may I introduce you to Scamper? Well, that is the unofficial name I have given him because he likes to scamper about." Mr. Scott gave a one-shoulder shrug. "Come here, buddy. It is not polite to jump on a lady." He scooped the animal into his arms without snagging her dress and tickled the white fur along the pup's cheek.

Keturah stepped closer to pet Scamper as well. "Is he yers?"

"No. He belongs to the Station Master, James Skaggs. But apparently, he is not suited as a hunting prospect, and he has quite taken to me. I have hope he will let me claim the dog when I leave."

Mr. Scott's smile dimmed for the quickest of moments. Was it due to Scamper's situation or his impending departure? Sadness twinged in her chest, though she had only just met the man. A thought struck her. Did he already have a family he planned to settle with? She took a step back. "Are ye leavin' soon?"

Another shrug and his smile was gone completely. "I suppose. Though I am not really sure where I will go."

Keturah tilted her head. "Ye have no plans of where to settle?"

"No. I was traveling with a group, but after I sustained an injury, I was left behind." His hand went to the back of his head as if to indicate where he had been hurt, but his golden-brown eyes took on a haunted look. It gave Keturah pause even as hope bloomed within her soul.

"So ye are travelin' alone?" She placed her hands behind her back and moved toward the clear, shimmering water of the creek as she attempted to feign mere curiosity.

Mr. Scott gave a nod as he lowered the pup to the ground. His brows were scrunched when he stepped up beside her. "Are you traveling alone as well?" He glanced behind her.

"Aye." Keturah paused, suddenly unsure how much she should share. Could it be this simple? Could God have led her to the man that would be the answer to her prayers before she had even reached the station? She could not know quite yet. There were still too many unanswered questions. "Though, by happenstance, me intended destination is James Skaggs's Station. I have some business there."

Mr. Scott's face broke into a beaming smile. "In that case, allow me to escort you the rest of the way." He turned and extended his arm as a proper gentleman would, causing a blush to creep into her cheeks. She slipped her arm into the crook of his elbow, keeping her touch light so she did not feel off-balance as she navigated the uneven terrain. If God did intend this man as her husband, she had a hunch that life with him would not be dull.

~

Keturah wrapped her hands around the warm mug of tea before her and took a deep breath, savoring the comforting aroma. As the warm spring day transitioned to a cool night, a low fire crackled in the hearth. And with her bones weary from travel, it was wonderful to be off her feet, seated at the kitchen table across from Mary Skaggs.

"So what exactly is it that brings you to our station?" Mary's eyes gleamed with curiosity, and her mouth pressed together in a suppressed smile.

Keturah was younger than every one of the other woman's seven children, all of whom had married and started their own families, and Mary had seemed glad for the female company since the moment she walked through the door. But the matriarch had kept her questions to a minimum until the men had disappeared to settle the animals for the night. Now, her inquiries could no longer be contained.

Keturah smiled and took a deep breath before she spilled the truth. "I am in need of a husband."

"Oh." Mary stopped with her mug halfway to her mouth and lowered it back to the heavy wooden table. "Need, not want?"

Keturah frowned as she gave a nod. "'Twas only me an' me father homesteadin' the land. An' last week, a tornado tore through our barn an' claimed his life. After all the hard work that we put into it the past couple of years, I dinnae want to lose the land. It is me home. An' so I need a husband, not only to protect me claim to the land, but to help rebuild the damage from the storm that took me father."

"That is quite the predicament," Mary agreed, frown lines creasing the tan skin around her mouth. "There are certainly plenty of young unattached men who have come west to make their way. But most have already begun their own homesteads. There could be some elder sons around that have not yet married."

"I did wonder about that."

Mary gave a thoughtful look as her gaze trailed to the door the men had exited through. Her eyes narrowed, and her finger tapped the side of her chin. "Though our guest, Daniel, is unattached and in need of land to settle." She raised her brows as she turned her attention back to Keturah.

"Aye. It did seem he would fit the bill." Her mouth

twisted, and her thumb rubbed over the smooth surface of the ceramic vessel in her hand. "How much do ye know of him?"

Mary took a moment to reply, causing apprehension to tingle up the back of Keturah's neck. What caused the woman's hesitancy? "James knows his situation better than I. I do know that the travel party left him behind after an incident during a river crossing. Though I am not privy to the circumstances, Daniel, his horse, and a small child were all injured."

Keturah nodded before her gaze fell to the dark liquid in her cup. Worry gripped her heart, even though she was well aware of how perilous river crossings could be. With every passing moment, it was becoming evident how much she would have to trust in the Lord's guidance in choosing a husband.

∾

*D*aniel could barely tear his gaze from the beautiful woman with flaming auburn hair seated to his right as he took another bite of venison.

Keturah glanced in his direction before she shoveled a forkful of potato into her mouth and turned her attention to their hosts, a brilliant blush coloring her freckled cheeks. "'Tis a wonderful meal, Mrs. Skaggs."

"Only simple noon-time fare." The middle-aged woman waved off the compliment with a smile.

The two women had sequestered themselves for a

private conversation after supper the night before, and curiosity gnawed at Daniel's insides. He had yet to learn what the young woman's business was at the station. Or how much longer he would be blessed with her company.

Mrs. Skaggs gave a wry smile as she glanced between him and Keturah, and suddenly, he understood what a trapped animal must feel. "Daniel, dear, you have not told us much about what brought you to Kentucky."

Daniel swallowed. He shrugged a shoulder before replying. "To find a home and make something of myself." Guilt roiled within, unsettling his stomach, as he withheld any detail that might paint him in a poor light.

Keturah glanced up at him, her green gaze both inquisitive and scrutinizing.

Somehow, it loosened his tongue. He sighed. His conscience would not allow him to conceal the truth from her. "I was an outsider within my own family. My mother died in childbirth when I was born, and my father blamed me for her death. A nanny was hired to see to my upbringing, and my brothers were banned from associating with me. In the end, my father arranged for my passage west and paid me to leave."

Keturah sucked in a breath. Then her hand came to rest on his forearm. Warmth spread through his arm at the weight of her touch through his shirt, and tears danced in her eyes. "I am sorry for that. I know what it is like to have yer father blame ye for yer mither's death."

In that moment, Daniel wanted to do nothing more than to pull her into his arms, to forget his own heartaches and to comfort the ones he saw reflected in the face before him. Suddenly, he understood why he was so drawn to this woman. Beneath her beauty was a kindred spirit.

Thoughts swirled through his mind as he stared down into her face. Ones that involved spending additional time with Keturah, coming to know her better. Even sharing a life with her. But his tender heart was running away with him. For what could he possibly offer a strong, capable woman such as her?

*May 16, 1782*

Keturah stalked back and forth along the creek bank where she had met Daniel only the day before. Pale stones crunched under foot and skittered across the ground. The gentle babble of the water would normally have provided a comfort to her anxious soul. But this morning, even with bright rays of sunshine filtering through the thick green foliage, serenity seemed elusive.

Instead, the decision that lay before Keturah had her restless, with her stomach in knots. Thus far, Daniel

Scott seemed every bit a kind, honest gentleman. After all, he had revealed the truth of his circumstances with her, despite how painful doing so must have been. But could he be the man she needed him to be? Would he be a helpmate in the repair and continuation of the homestead?

The knowledge of Daniel's upbringing left Keturah with more questions rather than less. Was it truly just an injury that kept him from continuing on with the travel party, or had he been unable to cut it on the frontier? Should she look farther from the station for another man better suited to the task? Her heart told her no. But could her heart be trusted? She had no experience in such matters to divine if it was the Lord's urging or if she was allowing herself to be swayed by a handsome face.

A rustle behind Keturah drew her attention, and she spun as Scamper came bounding out of a bush. She bent as he ran up to her and licked her cheek. "Why, hello, little fella."

Moments later, his owner came stalking out of the trees. His sad look disappeared when he saw her hunkered with the pup. Instead, a broad grin stretched across his face. One that warmed Keturah's heart and helped ease her indecision.

"He seems to have taken to you as well."

"Aye. It seems so." The thought brought a surprising sense of happiness. She smiled up at Daniel, a strange sensation filling her middle. Could this truly be the direction God was leading? A city boy who she would have to teach everything to? Her hesitation returned.

"Can I ask ye a question?" Keturah stood and stepped nearer to the tall man.

"Sure."

"Why were ye truly left behind? Was it only the injury?"

Daniel's face fell. "Oh."

With a sigh, he turned and started walking along the creek bank, and she fell into step beside him. For several moments, there was only the sound of the gurgling creek and twitter of birds. "The injury provided the travel party a good excuse to leave me behind. But it happened because I could not handle my horse." Self-loathing crept into his voice. "And it was not the first time. It was a miracle we had made it this far. I had failed more times than I could count. Each time camp was set, it seemed I required some sort of assistance. I was a hindrance, not a help, and I am still a bit amazed they had not left me behind before then. But this time, a little boy was hurt because of my inexperience. There was no way his parents could let me continue on, and I cannot blame them for that decision."

Keturah sucked in a breath. This was much more complicated than she had dreamed. Would Daniel be a hindrance to her as well? Maybe she should come clean regarding her own intentions. There was no reason to flounder in her pool of indecision if he had no interest in marrying her. "I suppose I should allow ye to know why I ask."

Daniel nodded. "Go ahead."

"A tornado claimed me father's life last week. I have no family, a barn that needs rebuildin', an' a homestead to keep up. We poured so much into the land over the past couple of years, I cannae imagine losin' it. So I need to take a husband. Someone to help protect me claim to the land an' work alongside me."

"Oh." Disappointment was evident in Daniel's voice, but his gaze did not waver from the ground before them. "That is quite the predicament. I hope you find the right husband."

Keturah stopped in her tracks and stared up at the man beside her. Was this his way of politely declining her? Scamper barked and jumped at her petticoats, but she ignored him as the sting of rejection settled in her chest.

Daniel turned toward her, his mouth pulled into a line and his expression apologetic. He stepped closer and touched her arm, his brown eyes boring deep into hers. "Keturah, you are beautiful and captivating. And your undertaking is admirable. Any man would be blessed to stand alongside you on the journey. I know we have not known one another long, but I am certain of that."

Heat rose up her neck. "Any man...but ye?"

Daniel's hand fell from her arm. "What?"

Keturah's own hands went to her hips. "Ye said any

man would be blessed to stand beside me. But evidently, ye have no desire to."

Daniel's brow scrunched as he looked down at her. "Wait. You wish for me to marry you?"

Keturah's shoulders sagged. Her head tilted to the side as she fought to understand where the miscommunication had happened. Or where Daniel's mind was. "That is why I was askin' why ye were left behind. Ye need land, an' I need a husband. But only if ye can pull yer weight."

Daniel seemed to stand a little taller. "Of course, I can pull my weight."

"Good." Keturah hesitated. "So…are we to marry, then?"

Daniel blew out a breath. "Do you desire a genuine marriage, with love, marital relations, and all that comes with?"

Keturah blinked. Did she? In that moment, it became clear that though she had decided to take a husband, she had not considered all it entailed. While Daniel was attractive and appeared to be a decent man, could she come to love him? After all, they barely knew one another. Butterflies swirled in her stomach.

"Keturah, this situation seems to be perfect for the both of us. But if I marry, I want a real, loving family, complete with children. And while I understand love would take time to grow, I do not want a marriage in name alone. I want to be able to hold my wife and kiss her. And I want us both to be committed to creating a loving, lasting relationship."

Keturah was dumbstruck. She had prayed for a loving helpmate. But now that one was standing before her, offering all the things she desired in a marriage, hesitation gripped her. She had proven over the last couple of years that she was capable of being so much more than a woman who kept house and tended to womanly duties. But was she capable of all those things as well as being a wife and mother? Her father's voice from when she was twelve came back to her. *Yer a woman. Ye'll never be good for nothin' but tendin' house an' raisin' bairns.* She swallowed the bile that threatened to rise and closed her eyes. Was she truly ready for this?

## CHAPTER 3

*May 17, 1782*

Daniel sighted down the length of his rifle the next day. "Lift the barrel a hair," James Skaggs whispered from behind him.

Daniel did as he was told, then sucked in a breath and pulled the trigger. Smoke and powder filled his vision. Before it cleared, another shot blasted near his right ear. Ears ringing, he turned to see Mr. Skaggs's rifle barrel pointed over his shoulder. And the deer lay on the ground. Though not by his hand. Daniel groaned.

"You will get it figured out, son." James clapped him on the shoulder.

Daniel's mouth pulled into a frown. *When* was the question. How could he provide for a family if he could not bring down game? Maybe it was a foolish daydream to believe he could have a loving family and a home where he was accepted and cared for. Settling a plot of land by himself, that was one thing. But becoming the head of household for a family before he had even learned the ropes of life beyond the mountains? That was a whole other story.

"What am I going to do?" He did not mean to say the question out loud, but as it so often happened, it slipped out of its own accord.

James turned to him. "You will learn." The simplicity and conviction in his words caught Daniel off guard.

"But how long will that take? Keturah needs me now."

Realization dawned on the older man's face. "Ahh. So that is the problem." He broke into a grin. James tucked his shotgun under his shoulder, facing away from Daniel. "Have the two of you come to an understanding, then?"

Daniel looked at the ground, giving the leafy green shrub near his foot a kick. "Since I had already agreed to come on the hunt with you today, we agreed she would take the day to consider her answer and let me know this afternoon when we return."

"I see." James nodded before he started walking toward the deceased deer. "And your recent failures are leaving you with some concerns."

Daniel followed, picking his way across the uneven earth covered in various plants and vines. A large brown one hung from the tree above him, and he ducked beneath. The Kentucky wilderness reminded him of what he imagined a jungle would have been like with its tall, dense foliage and strange flowers and animals at every turn. "Well, yes," he confided.

James chuckled. "Oh, son, you might as well lay that concern to rest now."

Daniel's brows pulled together as he stared at the man's back as he dodged a tree branch. "You do not think I should be concerned?" Considering what the man knew of his situation, that seemed unlikely.

James stopped and turned toward him as they reached the deer. Daniel could barely bring himself to look at the animal with its wide, staring eye and tongue hanging from its mouth. Another example of how he was unprepared. He glanced back up at the stationmaster, with his worn leather hat shielding deep blue eyes and black hair peppered with gray. His tan, lined face was a testament to his years and experience. "No man, or woman, is ever truly prepared for marriage. Marriage itself is an adventure, one that must be learned along the way. We are imperfect creatures, Daniel. Always making mistakes. You are not the first man to, and you will not be the last. You cannot allow the fear of failure to cause you to turn from something that could be the best choice you ever make. There is something so precious in marriage and family."

Daniel's lips pressed together. It could not be that simple. "But I know nothing of this life."

James let out another hearty laugh. "Very few of us do when we come west." He shook his head, a broad grin stretched across his face. "Sure, some are more prepared than others. But when your only options are survival or death, you would be surprised at how quickly a body catches on. Plus, you will not be alone in the matter. You will have Keturah. And having someone to share the journey with always makes it easier."

Daniel frowned down at the deer's tawny coat. Would it be easier, or would he be a disappointment? Yet again.

∽

The wind dashed Keturah's petticoats against her legs and whipped loose curls into her eyes as she watched the tree branches bending toward the east, their leaves turned upside down in invitation to the coming rain. She blinked against the sting. Without a doubt, a storm would be upon them soon. But where were the men?

She scanned the tree line beyond the station, her insides as restless and unsettled as the air around her. Memories of the night her father passed came flooding back to her. The relentless winds that beat rain against the cabin in thick, pounding sheets. The roar of the tornado as it tore through the barn. A shiver ran up her spine. *Lord, please dinnae let this be another storm like that one.*

Mrs. Skaggs stepped outside, arms wrapped around herself and mouth pulled into a line as she looked up at the darkening sky. "'Tis a'blowin' in."

Keturah nodded as her own lips pressed together. The first large droplet of rain plopped onto her shoulder, soaking through her blouse. Still, there was no sign of the men, only trees that swayed and bent. The rustle of the wind through their branches caused her insides to swirl. While it was normal for a hunt to last into the afternoon, should the men not have returned at the first sign of the changing weather?

"The men will be back any moment," Mrs. Skaggs assured her. The older woman gave her arm a pat as she turned to head back into the cabin. Keturah could barely manage a nod.

She had been sure her father would return any moment as well. After all, she had seen her massive father endure much worse than wind and rain. But the tornado had struck without warning. No one knew what life held from one moment to the next. She had learned that all too well.

Would God take Daniel from her too? The thought came from nowhere and caused her middle to tighten, though she barely knew the man.

Keturah blinked back tears and sucked in a deep breath of the warm air that blew without relenting. It had only been a little over two-and-a-half years since she had lost her mother and brother to the rushing river. And though her father had been cruel with his tongue and never believed in her worth, she still felt the sting of his loss. He had been her sole remaining family member. And now, she faced the prospect of losing the farm they had built. It was almost more than one person could bear.

Scamper whined from where he sat beside Keturah and peered up at her with big copper-colored eyes. She reached down and lifted the small pup into her arms, curling him into her chest. "'Twill be all right," she whispered, as much for herself as the animal.

Spinning, Keturah pushed the wooden door to the cabin open and moved inside. Surely, there was some task to be done that could occupy her mind. After lowering Scamper to the ground, she glanced about the room. Spotting the broom in the corner, she stalked over and took it in hand. Then she started vigorously sweeping the wood-plank floor. The motion kicked up a cloud of dust, making conditions in the already warm cabin nearly unbearable. She coughed and stopped long enough to wave a hand in front of her face. Meanwhile, Mrs. Skaggs hummed merrily as she rocked beside the hearth, mending her husband's shirt.

A twinge of guilt rippled through Keturah. Here she was causing the woman discomfort in her own home and instead of reprimanding her, Mrs. Skaggs showed an abundance of patience. It gave Keturah pause before she resumed her sweeping with a little less vigor. She simply could not sit still and remain serene like the

Skaggs matriarch. Nay, she needed to distract herself from the storm that raged outside.

She ought to be praying instead, but over the past couple of years, it seemed a chasm had opened between her and God. Most of the time, she wondered if He was even still listening. After all, there had been little evidence to the contrary. Instead, it seemed life had handed her disappointment after disappointment. Would it be such a surprise if this ended no differently? Had she somehow lost favor with her Heavenly Father as she had long ago done so with her earthly father?

But even as Keturah thought the words, Scamper's yipping bark at the door drew her attention, and her heart soared into her throat. She rushed to return the broom to its place, then hurried for the door. Scooping the pup up, she threw the door open. She squinted past the driving rain as Scamper squirmed in an attempt to escape her grip.

In the distance, at the edge of the meadow, the forms of two riders took shape, and a heavy weight lifted from her chest. Despite the fact that she was quickly becoming drenched from head to toe, she stood outside the cabin and awaited their slow approach. As they drew closer, it became clear the riders were indeed Daniel and Mr. Skaggs.

Nearing, Mr. Skaggs split off, the dead form of a deer draped over his saddle as he headed toward the barn. Meanwhile, Daniel continued on in her direction. Her heart picked up its pace, and a smile threatened to break her façade as she watched. Something about him riding toward her, as though he was coming home to her, felt so right. And in that moment, she no longer doubted what her answer would be when she gave it.

Her soon-to-be husband rode up to where she stood and slid from the saddle. Water dripped from his dark hair and down over his face, but he smiled at her despite it. "We need to tend to the deer and the horses, but we will speak later."

Keturah nodded. She could not form words. Part of her was relieved he was back in one piece, but the wind picked up and splattered rain against them, hinting that the storm was still growing. And now Daniel was going to the barn... "Be safe," she managed to whisper through the rain.

"Worried about me already?" He lifted a brow playfully, bringing a smile to her face.

"Only for Scamper's sake." Keturah was surprised at her ability to joke, but it brought a pleasant chuckle from the man before her. The warm sound eased a bit of the tension in her muscles.

Could this really be her future? Had God heard her and Margaret's prayers and answered them with a man who could bring a smile to her face in such worrisome circumstances? As Daniel led his horse away after Mr. Skaggs, her heart already felt lighter.

*D*aniel stepped from the stench-filled barn and inhaled deeply of the crisp, cool air that lingered after the storm. However, the sensation did little to quell his unsettled spirit. Pink painted the sky over the darkened tree line before giving way to the vast expanse of purple night overhead, signaling the calm after the storm. At least, Daniel prayed it was so.

Was it the blood and guts of preparing the deer or the anticipation of his conversation with Keturah that had his midsection in knots? While she had seemed pleased at his return, as though she might have even been concerned for his welfare, he could not be sure if she would agree to his ideal of marriage. He had experienced far too much rejection in his life to believe that she would willingly accept the arrangement. In fact, her interest had shocked him to begin with, so much so that he had not understood her implication at first.

A grin stretched Daniel's lips as a breeze ruffled his hair. Keturah's spirit had sure come out when she thought he was not interested. Her attitude had hinted at a fire within that burned as brightly as her flaming auburn locks. And he found it both refreshing and intriguing.

"Time for supper, son." James gripped his shoulder as he passed, and Daniel's stomach churned. He was uncertain if he could keep a meal down at the moment, no matter how hungry he was. Still, he followed James toward the man's home, the tension in his body increasing with each step. Would he be rejected and left behind once again?

Daniel swallowed as James opened the door. Crossing over the threshold, Daniel scanned the room, his gaze landing on Keturah where she stood by the fire. Immediately, she turned in his direction, and a smile brightened her face. Praying her reaction was a good sign, Daniel glanced toward James and Mary. "Mrs. Skaggs, I am quite sure you have prepared another delicious meal, but I was hoping I could have a moment with Keturah before we partake."

The middle-aged woman gave him a knowing smile that crinkled the edges of her dark eyes. "Of course. Just do not be long."

Keturah moved gracefully and confidently across the room and slipped her hand into the crook of his arm when he offered it, though her eyes held a hint of the fear that coiled deep within him. The night air was a refreshing and welcome change as they stepped outside, the last bit of color having slipped from the sky.

Silence stretched between them in an agonizing torture, so Daniel filled it with the first thought that came to mind. "I find the air most pleasant tonight. How about you?"

Keturah glanced up at him with a brow raised and one corner of her mouth quirked up. "Aye. 'Tis nice."

Daniel fished for more words. "Our hunt was successful as well. James brought in a deer."

"Aye. Always a blessin'."

Daniel almost groaned as the silence returned. While the conversation was not going well, he could not bring himself to utter the words that would change his life, for better or worse. Above them, stars speckled the now partially clear sky. He should return Keturah to the cabin before she caught a chill. But that meant confronting the inevitable.

Swallowing his fears, he stopped and turned toward her. Her pale, freckled face shone brightly in the dark night as she looked expectantly up at him, that little smile still tugging at the edges of her mouth. "Daniel, are ye goin' to ask the question on yer mind?"

His mouth dropped open before he recovered his senses and a laugh escaped. This woman was quite the breath of fresh air. He sucked in a breath of his own and forced the words from his mouth. "Keturah, would you do me the honor of becoming my wife?"

The little smile stretched into a broad grin, easing the tension in his middle. "Aye. If ye will have me." Her head dipped in a nod.

All the air left his lungs. Keturah was inquiring if he would accept *her*? With all her beauty and spirit? As confident and capable as she appeared? When had anyone ever asked for his acceptance, instead of the other way around? "Of course." The words rushed out.

The radiant joy reflected upon Keturah's countenance was enough to make any male swoon. And not only that, but her entire being relaxed, as though she had felt a taste of the same turmoil as he.

He smiled down at her as he turned and offered his arm again. "Miss Elliot, may I have the pleasure of escorting you back to the Skaggs's residence? Perhaps they can aid us in establishing the details of when and where we are to wed."

Soft laughter drifted to him on the night air as Keturah wrapped her hand around his arm a tad tighter than before. "Aye. I am sure they shall." Warmth seeped through Daniel as he slipped his right hand atop hers, relishing in the feel of her skin against his. Could this truly be happening? It seemed impossible that he was walking with the woman who would become his wife, that he would make a life with. Finally, his dream of a loving family seemed within his grasp.

# CHAPTER 4

*May 18, 1782*

"Careful." Keturah grimaced and reached out to her husband as he slipped on the muddy embankment behind her. The creek they were about to cross was shallow, but the hillsides flanking it were covered in rocks and boulders. Daniel caught himself on one such gray boulder and returned to an upright position before she could latch onto his arm. Behind her, Cinnamon carefully picked her way down to the water's edge. Scamper had already traveled the path and lapped at the crystal-clear water near Keturah's feet. Satisfied that everyone was well, Keturah turned and sloshed through the cool liquid and started picking her way up the far bank.

Thankfully, they were nearly home. Even with a horse, travel had taken longer with the addition of her companions, and the golden sunlight of later afternoon slanted down through the canopies of the trees. But this was the last rise before they reached the valley where the cabin lay. If she could safely escort her new family members up this steep path and over the hill, they would be free to settle into their new surroundings. And their new relationship.

A tingle of both apprehension and anticipation rose up Keturah's spine as she considered what the night might hold for her and Daniel. Their wedding had been a simple ceremony at the home of a reverend near the station that morning. Warmth spread through her cheeks as she considered the kiss they had shared at its closure. Though timid at first, the gesture had been much sweeter and more enticing than anything she had ever imagined. But, much to her relief, Daniel had not pressed her for any kind of physical contact since. Sure, he would place a hand at her elbow or the small of her back. Their connection had remained rather comfortable and casual. But how long would that last? Considering her husband wanted a marriage in every way, would he be patient enough to allow love to grow slowly between them?

Forgetting to watch her step, she stepped on a slick, exposed root, and her ankle twisted as her foot slipped free. She hissed in pain, then continued on, being sure to pay more attention to her surroundings.

But Daniel was at her side in a flash, his touch warm on her arm through the thin fabric of her bodice. "Are you hurt?" His dark brows were lowered over stormy brown eyes.

Keturah smiled, his concern touching, if a bit amusing. Never had anyone she knew worried over such a small matter. "Nay. I am well," she assured him. Though there was a twinge in her ankle with each step, it was nothing she could not ignore. She had endured much worse. And on the Kentucky frontier, a person had to keep pushing on. In fact, only a few months prior, she had stitched up her own hand after an incident in the kitchen. And removed the same stitches herself a week later. This slip of a step would not cause a moment's hesitation on her part.

"If you are sure." Daniel seemed hesitant to release his grip on her arm.

"I am," she reiterated before turning back the direction they were headed. Scamper scurried ahead of her, up the hillside.

"What are those?"

Keturah closed her eyes and took a deep breath, forcing her fingers to relax around Cinnamon's reins before she turned her attention to Daniel. With the mare laden down with his plentiful belongings, her husband had been unable to safely ride double. After putting his heel in the mare's flank for the third time, and subsequently falling off her rear when she bolted forward, he had kindly offered to walk. And at times such as this, when the trail had become too steep, Keturah herself had dismounted and led the animal.

She followed the direction of Daniel's pointing finger to where little white flowers dotted the hillside, nearly hidden amongst the other greenery. "That is foamflower." Keturah attempted to keep her voice calm as she replied.

"Beautiful, is it not?" Daniel turned a broad grin in her direction, but the gesture only slightly abated her frustration. How was one person capable of asking so many questions? Since they had departed from Skaggs's Station that morning, she had provided the names of more trees, plants, and birds than she could count. Though she was glad Daniel was interested in the land they would call home, she much preferred to enjoy the peace of nature silently. Maybe it had come from spending the past two years with her father, when the best course of action seemed to have been to always keep her mouth shut.

But her patience was wearing thinner the closer to home they grew. Home. After several days away, she longed for its familiarity and comfort. Perhaps her life would not feel quite so upside down once she settled back into her normal tasks and routines.

Suddenly, Daniel stopped and placed his hand on her arm. Exasperated, she turned once again. But her husband stood frozen, his gaze anchored on a spot several yards ahead of them. "Stay still," he advised quietly, his tone serious.

Keturah's brows lowered before she followed the direction of his gaze. Between two trees, a coyote stood, watching them warily. She could not help the chuckle that escaped her throat. Meanwhile, beside her, Scamper noticed as well and proceeded to yap incessantly.

"Keturah," Daniel snapped in a quiet whisper. "This is not a time for laughter. We need to run or hide. To protect ourselves somehow. Scamper, hush, you will get us all killed." He reached for the rifle tucked into the scabbard on the side of the saddle, but Keturah put a hand atop his to stay it.

"Nay." She shook her head as she swallowed the giggles that rose from within. "That is only a coyote. He is more scared of ye than ye are of him. See?" She gestured up the hill where the canine was already padding away. Scamper grinned happily up at her as though he had been victorious at protecting them from some fearsome beast. Cinnamon simply stomped and snorted as though she were bored with the entire ordeal.

Daniel looked about at the three of them, then back to where the coyote had disappeared. His lips pressed together, and a wrinkle marred his brow. "You are sure it was not a wolf?"

Keturah chuckled again before she could stop herself. "Aye. I am sure." As she turned to continue up the hill, her mouth still twisted in a suppressed grin. Her husband had much to learn about this land.

∽

## REVERENCE IN THE WILDERNESS

*B*efore them lay a beautiful valley, marked by a large cabin, two expansive plots of turned soil, and what one could only assume had once been the barn. Daniel grimaced at the sight of its mangled remains, his heart aching for his wife as he considered the devastation that must have coursed through her upon finding her father within. Instinctively, he reached toward her. Much to his delight and surprise, she willingly took his hand.

"This is home," she breathed, her voice swelling with pride.

"It will be my honor and privilege to make a home here with you," Daniel reassured Keturah. While this remote life of toil and strife was much different from anything he had imagined growing up, he did indeed mean the words. After all those years of isolation and rejection, to have someone to care for and create a life alongside was a blessing. No matter how difficult that livelihood would be.

Together, he and Keturah made their way down the hillside. She spoke up once they had arrived before the cabin. "Let us unload Cinnamon. Then I will take her to the creek to water her an' fetch some meat for supper from the springhouse."

"You have a second house?" The words were out of Daniel's mouth before he knew it, and he immediately regretted their release. When would he stop embarrassing himself by speaking without giving thought to his words? For now, as Keturah peered at him over the horse's back, he could see exactly how foolish she believed him to be. Heat burned him from the inside out.

"Nay. We do not. The springhouse is where we keep meat an' vegetables to keep them cool, so they will last."

Daniel frowned. "Oh." Without any additional comments that could earn him further disapproval, he began to relieve Cinnamon of her many burdens. The mare flicked her tail impatiently while she waited, and another twinge of guilt shot through him. On the journey west, his mount had been more heavily laden that even those of families who should have had more belongings and supplies than he. And to make matters worse, most of the items were personal in nature, rather than those required to survive on the frontier.

As Keturah carried leather pouches and carpetbags alongside him, it started to sink in how frivolous many of the items would seem now—though the leather case filled with books would always be a treasured possession, one he hoped his wife would come to appreciate as well. She spoke not a word as they carried the items inside and gathered them in a pile in the middle of the spacious cabin. Keturah had spoken little on the trip home, and he was beginning to get the notion that she was simply a woman of few words.

When Cinnamon was fully unloaded, she turned and led the mare away. Scamper sat beside him, tongue hanging out as he grinned up at Daniel. The pup glanced between him and Keturah as if inquiring if they should follow her. Daniel looked from the dog to Keturah's retreating back. Maybe the dog was right.

He needed to learn the lay of the land and how things were done so that he could be of assistance to his wife. So that he could ease the burden on the shoulders of the beautiful woman whose auburn locks captured the golden sunlight as she moved farther away. Before she reached the edge of the woods, he jogged after her. Scamper followed his example, dashing by him in a blur of brown and white to catch up with Keturah.

"Keturah," Daniel called as he quickly covered the ground with his long stride. But at his and Scamper's sudden appearance, Cinnamon twisted and backed away from Keturah, straining against the reins. His wife hissed as the leather slipped through her hands. The whites of his mare's eyes showed as she took in the newcomers, her nostrils flaring.

"Whoa, mare." Anger and impatience laced Keturah's voice. "Whoa, mare." Her words took on a gentler tone as she repeated them, taking slow, measured steps toward Cinnamon, her gaze averted and her hand outstretched. The horse let out several more audible puffs of air before she allowed Keturah within reach. His wife ran her hand up her soft, chestnut-colored nose to her forehead and slipped it under the animal's forelock. Cinnamon lowered her head, pressing into her touch and licking her lips as she visibly relaxed. Finally, Keturah turned, her green gaze cutting into him.

"I am sorry. I did not mean to startle Cinnamon," Daniel apologized.

"Well, ye need to be more careful next time," Keturah snapped. "Horses can be easily spooked. An' with ye runnin' up behind her like that, she coulda kicked ye an' killed ye." The glare she sent him did not appear to hold an ounce of worry, though, only anger. But what should he expect? They barely knew one another, and likely, her primary concern was that she might lose the husband she had only just gained. One who was supposed to make her life easier, not almost get himself killed.

Daniel let out a sigh as he fell into step with their misfit family.

A short distance into the woods, they came upon a creek that cut through the valley, fed by a natural spring. There, Keturah handed him the reins. "Hold them here, where she is able to reach the water. But dinnae let her go if she spooks." She shot another withering glance his way.

Daniel nodded and did as she instructed. As the mare lowered her head to the crystal-clear water, Keturah made her way over to what appeared to be another small cabin. He frowned as she disappeared inside. This was certainly not how he had anticipated their first afternoon at home proceeding. How was he supposed to win his wife's favor when she continually had to correct him as one would a child? He had to find a way to do better.

When Keturah reemerged with her arms laden with meat and potatoes, he led the mare behind her back to the cabin.

"'Twill be best to put the mare in the corral outside the barn until we can rebuild." Keturah nodded toward a fenced-in area next to the rubble. The structure seemed to have already been repaired, and inside stood a cow munching on grass. Pride swelled within his chest. His wife was quite resourceful and tenacious. Daniel loosed the mare inside the corral without mishap. Then he hooked the mare's bridle over a fence-post and followed Keturah into the house.

When he entered, she was bent at the hearth, starting a fire. Once it began to crackle to life, she gave it a little coaxing, blowing upon the flame before she moved to the table to begin peeling and cutting the potatoes.

Daniel watched, feeling completely out of place. "How can I be of assistance?" He moved to stand beside the table near his wife.

Keturah stopped chopping and gestured toward the pile of items in the middle of the room with the knife in her hand. "If ye want to begin unpackin', I can tell ye where yer things should go while I tend to the cookin'."

Daniel nodded before he walked over and lifted a carpetbag from the edge of the stack. After setting it on the bed tucked beneath the loft, he opened it and withdrew the tiny leather pouch that was nestled atop his clothing. He lifted the flap and extracted a small golden band. The diamonds within it were set in the shape of a flower, and the metal worker had manipulated the gold on either side into intricate roses. He chanced a glance in the direction of his wife. Keturah cut the potatoes in quick, rhythmical slices that belied years of practice. Though they had been married that morning, Daniel had chosen to reserve the ring his childhood nanny had entrusted to his care before he left home. It had been her mother's, and he wanted the moment to be special when he offered it to his wife. Before now, Nanny had been the only person in his life to ever show him love. But as Keturah focused on the task before her without even glancing in his direction, he wondered if that would actually change.

# CHAPTER 5

*May 18, 1782*

Keturah bit the inside of her lip as she settled the pan full of meat and potatoes over the fire. Scamper whimpered in his sleep from where he dozed near the warm hearth. The full day's travel had tuckered out the young pup.

She straightened and flicked a glance in Daniel's direction. He was placing what she hoped was the last of his clothing alongside her and her father's in the wardrobe. Additional garments were not likely to fit within the piece of furniture that had gone from relatively bare to full to the brim within minutes. Though it was strange her husband possessed more clothing than she, Keturah attempted to rein in her judgmental thoughts.

It was time that she showed her husband some

grace over circumstances he could not control. Her treatment of him since they arrived home had been quite harsh considering his naïveté was not his fault. A thread of guilt swirled in her stomach as she watched him. The corners of his mouth pulled down into a frown.

Keturah tilted her head. Had she contributed to that expression, or did another issue weigh on his mind? Either way, she was his wife now, and it was her responsibility to ease his burdens. In fact, rather than focus on how frivolous his many clothes were, maybe it was time she refashioned some of her father's clothing into items she could wear, thereby expanding her own options. Though most of her father's old garments were stained and threadbare.

"Where should I place these books?" Daniel's shift to another topic jerked her from her thoughts. She refocused her gaze on where he stood now with a leather satchel in hand.

"Books?" Keturah stepped closer. Though she enjoyed reading, her father had thought reading to be a waste of precious time. So she only owned one small volume which once belonged to her mother.

"Yes. I quite enjoy reading, and there were several books I could not bear to part with." Daniel opened the pack to show her the contents.

She sucked in a breath. Rather than the handful she had imagined, there were more than a dozen volumes inside. What an incredible blessing. Her heart warmed as she smiled up at her husband. A new respect for him bloomed. Their children would be well provided for in the way of literature.

Keturah stopped herself. Where had that thought come from? While Daniel had made it clear he wanted children, it would still be a time yet before love grew and children came. Right?

"Keturah?"

Her gaze darted to Daniel's face. His brows rose in question. The books...

"Oh, um..." She glanced around. "We will need to build a bookcase for them. Perhaps some of the broken timbers from the barn can be cut down to be of use."

Daniel hesitated before he gave her a small, tight smile. "Yes. That should work just fine." He nodded, but something in his demeanor gave Keturah pause.

Was he trying to convince her or himself? Was it the task of building the bookcase that concerned him? A wealthy upbringing would mean he had never had the need to build his own furniture. Ah, well, they would figure it out. Together. If she kept telling herself that, surely, it would come true.

"Do you like to read?" Daniel's question competed with the sizzling of the food.

Keturah darted over to the hearth but spoke as she knelt and stirred. "Aye. I do."

Daniel leaned the satchel against the wall near the wardrobe and came to crouch beside her. His hand rested on her elbow, and she tried to ignore the warmth.

Surely, it was from the fire. "You know we are married now. What is mine is yours. You can read any of the books you wish, as often as you desire."

When Keturah turned toward Daniel, the fire reflected in his golden-brown eyes, and she had to swallow as her mouth went dry. "I appreciate it." For some reason, her words came out in a whisper. She ducked her gaze back down to the food. Food. Stirring. That was safe ground, away from the new sensations that coursed through her. Was it normal to feel this way around one's husband? So unnerved and off-kilter? She much preferred to be in full control of her faculties.

But Daniel hovered there, his breath so near her ear. Her heart quickened its pace. Keturah swallowed. She stirred the venison and potatoes a moment longer before she cleared her throat. "Did ye finish puttin' all yer belongin's away?"

"Yes. Is there another task I can assist with?"

Keturah racked her brain. "Ye could set out a couple of plates an' forks. They are on the shelf there." She gestured with the wooden spoon in her hand, and Daniel moved to comply with her request. Keturah let out a breath. Being a married woman was going to take some adjusting to.

*D*aniel doubted a single speck of dust lingered within the cabin. After tending to the dishes, Keturah had taken to cleaning every surface within their home. Though he could not tell, she claimed that the cabin had gathered dust in her absence. And she had attacked it vigorously.

Daniel stood, unsure of what to do with himself. His belongings were all put away, Scamper had been convinced to take a short walk, and there was only one broom that he could tell. "Is there any way in which I can be of assistance?"

Keturah shook her head and continued her aggressive sweeping. Daniel frowned. Had he done something to offend his wife so that she was avoiding coming to bed? Suddenly, it struck him. This was their wedding night. She was married to someone she barely knew, and considering his speech about wanting a true marriage in every sense of the word, she likely expected him to require her to fulfill her wifely duties.

Daniel let out a relieved sigh and padded up behind his wife, placing a hand at her elbow. "Keturah?"

She turned to look up at him, her light-green eyes wide.

He gentled his voice. "Stop cleaning. Come to bed."

Keturah visibly swallowed.

He chuckled and shook his head. "I do not expect anything tonight. I told you that I knew love would take time to grow. I expect everything else will come along with it in time. Tonight, I only wish to share a warm bed with my new wife... if you are amenable to that."

Keturah glanced from him to the bed and back, her foot fidgeting under her petticoats, swishing the fabric against his leg while her grip on the broom remained steadfast. Finally, she gave him a nod. He reached out and carefully eased the broom handle from her hand. He returned it to where it had been propped beside the hutch. But when he turned back around, his wife had disappeared.

Daniel sighed. Maybe he really had failed in some way serious enough that Keturah did not wish to even share her bed with him. Should he find another arrangement? Lay some quilts upon the floor? Maybe that would show Keturah that he was earnest in giving her time and space. He sighed and moved to the chest at the end of the bed. It seemed his nights on the hard ground were not over. But he would do what it took, for his wife. He pulled several quilts from the chest and placed them on the ground, then began to ready for bed.

Keturah opened the door and stopped at the sight of him shedding his vest. "Are ye not goin' to sleep in the bed?" Her brows lowered.

"I thought you did not want..."

Keturah shook her head. "I only went to tend to personal matters." Her voice was stern and defensive.

Daniel sighed. Him and his propensity to jump to

conclusions. He scrubbed a hand over his face. "That makes sense. I am sorry."

He started to fold the quilts and was surprised when Keturah came over to help him. When she brought her end of the partially folded blanket up to meet his, she met his gaze. His heart picked up its pace as he took in her sun-freckled face. Slowly, he reached out and brushed a curl away. Maybe love would truly grow, if only he and wife could convene on the same page.

~

M*AY* 19, 1782

Keturah looked up at the sky as she stopped pulling timber from the wreckage of the barn to drag an arm across her forehead. The sun had nearly reached its peak, and still she worked alone. Anger surged through her, fueling her ability to lift the heavy beams. Beams which she should have assistance in moving.

Not only had she already toiled for hours planting corn that morning, but now she worked to clear rubble so the barn could be rebuilt in the same location. All the while, her husband continued to slumber. Was a woman supposed to summon her husband from bed? Keturah dropped the broken beam on the ground several feet away and frowned.

Her only experience with such matters had come

from observing her parents. And her mother had never had to rouse her father. If he had not awakened to the smell of breakfast cooking, it had indicated an illness that kept him bedridden. In fact, while Keturah was nearly always the first to stir, the rest of her family had never been long behind her. As soon as the sun had risen over the horizon, the entire Elliot clan would soon be awake if they were not already.

Keturah smiled at the memory of working alongside her mother in the garden one day before the move, back in Virginia. The dew had lingered on the tomatoes and squash as they picked them. As they worked, the sun had cut through the mist with its bright, warm rays, replacing the muggy morning with a stifling hot day. There was something special about experiencing those first precious hours of the day. To watch a new beginning, blessed by the Lord.

Last night, after Daniel had been so understanding in giving her the time and space she needed, while butterflies fluttered in her stomach, she had felt that same hope for her marriage. If only she could recapture that feeling now.

Back at the debris pile, she attempted to lift another timber. But as she stood with the squared-off log hoisted onto her shoulder, she swayed. Whether her husband arose to join her or not, she needed sustenance to continue working. Keturah dropped the beam back into the rubble before she swiped her arm across her forehead again. Then she rubbed her hands down her aproned front and turned toward the house.

Entering the stuffy cabin, she propped the door open wide to allow the sunshine and a breeze to filter through. She threw open the shutters covering the windows. Though it was still May, the day had proven to be quite warm.

Plus, her soul needed light and fresh air. Keturah had never preferred remaining shut inside in the dark cabin while her brother and father were free to work outside. It had been another reason time spent in the garden with her mother had been so precious. She had even found joy in the times when she and Ma would labor over the washtub outside on a nice day. There was simply something about the sunshine that fed her soul.

Keturah glanced to where her husband remained in bed, his arm flopped above his head. Collecting two plates from the hutch her father had built, she settled them onto the table with a clatter. The man did not move a muscle. In fact, a contented snore arose from the bed.

Keturah's hands went to her hips. Then she turned her attention to the uneaten plate of breakfast still waiting on the table. Should she make him a cold sandwich when there was already food available to him? It seemed such a waste to let the meal spoil. But at least the pig would enjoy the treat. Dutifully, she sliced bread and ham for both plates before dusting her hands on her apron and looking at her husband once more.

She marched across the room to the bedside, and though she had already done so several times that morning, laid a hand on his forehead. Reassured that he had not taken ill, she bent and gave the man's slumbering form a shake. "Daniel," she all but yelled.

He jerked awake and glanced about wide-eyed. "Wha-what is it?" He scrubbed a hand over his face, then looked around again as he sat up, as though there must be some danger for her to awaken him so.

"What is it? It is nearly noon!"

Daniel blinked up at her. "I am so sorry, Keturah. You should have awakened me." He stood, shirtless, and placed a hand on her arm as he looked down into her face, his eyes full of apology. The same strange sensation from the night before settled into her middle.

"I was not sure if ye would want me to." She offered her own sort of apology.

"Yes, please. I must have been tired from our journey, but I do not wish to pose any inconvenience to you or leave you without the help you need. We have a farm to save." He flashed that bright smile of his, the one that had caught her attention and pulled her closer from that first day.

"Aye. We do," she agreed, hope working its way back into her heart. The day was not a complete loss, after all. There were still plenty of hours before dark for her and Daniel to work alongside one another, clearing the rubble.

Daniel squeezed her arm affectionately before she

stepped away, giving him one last lingering look. Taking in the sight of her new husband shirtless, with his dark hair mussed from sleep, her insides swirled. He certainly was a handsome man, not rotund in the slightest or scruffy as her father had been.

But would that be enough? While an attraction between husband and wife should ease the union, Daniel had already proven that he might be as much hindrance as help. Keturah sighed. She should not judge the man so harshly. It would take time for him to learn the intricacies of frontier life. But he was willing and eager. Was that not what mattered the most? A person could learn what they did not know. And if love grew between them...

The corner of her mouth tipped upward at the thought.

# CHAPTER 6

*D*aniel stepped outside into the sunshine and immediately adjusted the kerchief at his neck. It was the warmest day he had experienced in Kentucky thus far, and Keturah was already at the rubble of the tornado-stricken barn, working to clear the broken timbers. His heart ached to see her take on such work. It spurred him into action as he moved alongside her, lifting a beam from the pile.

But when Keturah looked up, her brows pulled together. "Ye do not need a waistcoat an' all workin' in this heat. Ye will only ruin it. Me father most often worked in his shirtsleeves."

Pausing, Daniel glanced down at his attire. Out of habit, he had dressed as he had each day on the trail, only neglecting his coat due to the heat. But Keturah was right. Not only was summer pushing spring out, but they would be partaking in tough, manual labor that could easily damage his clothing. Not to mention that it was only him and his wife in the valley. If she was comfortable seeing him in his shirtsleeves, it would make sense to dress appropriately for the work and weather. "True."

Daniel turned back to the house, mentally kicking himself as he went. Why had he not thought his choice through before he stepped outside?

Quickly, Daniel shed the extra clothing items and tossed them upon the bed. Then he darted back out to assist his wife. *Wife.* The word made him smile. While their relationship was not one born of love, he longed for the loving family he had never experienced. At least Keturah had somewhat accepted him when she took him in marriage. Now he only had to prove himself. And he was off to a rocky start.

But he was determined, so he dove into the work with Keturah. Despite how his muscles ached and sweat trickled down his back, he relished the togetherness of them working side by side, moving beam after beam. This was how a man and wife were meant to be. Their camaraderie would provide the foundation upon which their love could be built. Plus, if he could show his wife he was reliable, maybe she would learn to trust him with her affections.

Slowly, they cleared the damage inflicted by the tornado. Though how much harm had the disaster done within Keturah? Not only had it taken her last remaining relative and left him for her to find among the rubble, but it had placed her in a hopeless situation that had driven her to marry a practical stranger. Daniel chanced a glance in her direction, but there was no reading her stoic expression, so focused was she on the task at hand.

"Once we clear the damage, we will begin to rebuild?"

Keturah frowned in his direction before she swept her gaze over the sea of splintered wood. "Aye," she agreed and bent for another beam.

"How do you get wood out here?" Daniel lifted a timber onto his shoulder and followed her.

Keturah raised an eyebrow. "The trees." She stretched the word out, indicating he should have known.

Daniel grimaced inwardly. But how would they get the wood cut down into these beams? "Do you have the tools needed to square them off?"

Keturah's frown deepened, and her forehead creased in thought. "Aye. Father knew how to use them. I have watched him but was never taught meself. The timbers dinnae have to be squared off or flattened, though. We can built it with rough logs. Then the only difficulty will be the notches so that they lock into one another. But that can be done with an ax." She shrugged a shoulder.

She feigned nonchalance, but realization swept over Daniel. Keturah had been in search of a husband who was more knowledgeable than her. Someone who could build her a sturdy barn. Instead, she was stuck with him. Daniel swallowed.

"We will figure it out," he assured her. Though inside, he prayed the words were true.

~

Keturah gently closed the door behind her and stopped to take a deep breath of the cool night air. The refreshing feel of it against her cheeks was a welcome change from the suffocating cabin. While her husband was trying to be helpful, she might have started climbing the walls had she not excused herself for a moment.

After hours spent sifting through the rubble, separating broken timbers from wood and objects that could still be of use, Daniel had asked to see the tools her father used to turn rough timber into usable beams. Answering his plethora of questions, she explained what she had witnessed and how she thought the process would go. Now, the man still seemed obsessed with the subject as he bent over page after page, drawing out specifics for the rebuild in a notebook he had brought with him on his journey eastward. Though she doubted a single one of his ideas would work. How could someone who knew nothing of double-pen barns devise a plan of how to construct one? Daniel was not even a carpenter by trade. Many times, she had urged him to agree to build a simple, rough-hewn barn. But

Daniel was insistent that she should have the same quality of barn that had stood before.

Keturah shook the thoughts from her mind and stepped into the dim light of a half moon. Crickets chirped all around her as the dew clung to her petticoats and bullfrogs croaked in the distance. Out here, the world was at peace.

As her heart and mind began to settle, she walked over to the corral where Cinnamon grazed near the fence. Keturah rested her forearms atop the top rail and watched the mare pick at the damp grass. After a moment, the animal ventured over to ensure she had not brought anything more enticing to munch on. "Sorry, girl. No apple tod—" Her apology died on her lips when, as she shifted, her boot knocked into an object that made a clinking sound.

Brows pulled together, she bent to identify the source of the sound. Her hand clasped onto Cinnamon's damp bridle, where it lay in a heap on the ground. But as she lifted it, her confusion turned to ire. For the moonlight revealed the headstall had been chewed right through. Until she could find the time to fashion a new one from some of the old leather harness they'd recovered that morning, the bridle was completely useless. Tears formed in Keturah's eyes, and she slapped the item against her side and shook her head. Thanks to her husband's naiveté, that was one more task added to her endless to-do list.

She bit her lip to keep the tears from falling. How

could this be God's plan for her? How could it be that when all she desired was to save the homestead, He had brought her a partner who was more of a hassle than a helpmate?

~

May 26, 1782

"Scamper! No!" Keturah dropped her seed pouch and brought one knee up as the pup dashed after a squirrel. Both animals went careening toward the tree line. At the end of the row, Daniel chuckled. She frowned at him from where she knelt in the dirt. "It is not funny. He is goin' to chase away all me squirrels."

One corner of her husband's mouth lifted in a grin, and his gaze took on a mischievous gleam. "*Yer* squirrels?"

Keturah shrugged a shoulder and diverted her attention back to dropping cucumber seeds every so far in the little trench Daniel had hug with the pick ax. "I enjoy watchin' 'em play as I work in the mornin's." She lifted both her gaze and a brow at her husband. "I listen to the birds a'singin' as well."

Daniel glanced around the valley they called home. The late-morning sun had pushed out the thick fog of earlier and dried the last of the dew. Purple and white wildflowers peeped out from the tall grass near the trees. "It is quite peaceful here. I understand why so many people want to come west."

Finishing out the row of cucumbers, Keturah dusted her hands on her apron and moved beside her husband. Varieties of trees, now full and green, filled the hillsides that rose up on either side of them. Several yards away, a red-breasted robin hopped about in search of worms. Meanwhile, Scamper's squirrel chattered away from the treetop, angry that its search for whirligigs had been interrupted. The corners of her mouth lifted. "Aye. There is little better than a Kentucky mornin'. 'Cept for maybe the sky painted red at sunset."

Beside her, Daniel's stomach rumbled. "And maybe a nice meal."

Keturah chuckled. Her husband might ask a million questions, but he was rather easy to get along with. "I suppose I could feed ye," she teased and bumped her shoulder against his. Then, with his hand at the small of her back, they headed toward the cabin.

Daniel stopped when they neared and turned back toward the meadow, cupping his hands around his mouth. "Scamper!"

The puppy peeped out of the trees, and when Daniel called again, he shot across the clearing toward them. His little white legs pumped energetically, and his tongue hung from his mouth. With a smile in place, Keturah turned and stepped up onto the porch.

She gasped at the sudden sensation of water splattering against the back of her neck. Her shoulders scrunched up toward her ears before she turned to her husband, who stood beside the barrel of rainwater that sat at the corner of their home.

"I did nothing." Though he held his hands up in front of his chest, the humor dancing across his face told a different story.

Keturah stepped to the edge of the porch. With the extra height, she could, for once, look Daniel in the eye without tilting her head upward. "Ye know, I reserve the right to withhold meals."

Daniel moved closer, his face hovering inches from hers. The corner of his mouth lifted. "You could...but I know where you keep the food. I could simply prepare my own meals."

The heat in his eyes caused her insides to turn to mush. Keturah swallowed, and her gaze fell to his mouth. All thoughts of a retort slipped from her mind.

They had been married a week. A kiss would be more than acceptable, right? Daniel's hand slipped around her waist, and it was all the encouragement she needed. Her lips pressed to his. The kiss was gentle and tentative, but sweet and tantalizing. Craving more, Keturah leaned into her husband and deepened their kiss, spreading her hands against his sturdy chest. Daniel responded in kind, hugging her to him. She could lose herself there, in his embrace. Instead, she pulled back and gazed into his face, her cheeks flaming.

This marriage proved more surprising at every turn.

*June 1, 1782*

Keturah pushed soft dirt over the last in a row of beets and sat back on her heels. She dusted her hands on her old stained apron and closed her eyes on a sigh. One more item on her list complete. A warm breeze brushed her cheeks and lifted an errant curl near her face. Sliding it back, she cast her gaze toward the steady scrape of the plane over a twelve-foot log. Daniel worked with his shirtsleeves rolled above his elbows and the top two buttons of his shirt undone. Despite the mild morning, sweat beaded on his brow.

With a smile upon her lips, Keturah rose and walked over to where he worked several feet away. Slowly, his movements with the hand plane removed the rounded portion of the log, transforming it into a squared-off timber that would be added to the base of the new barn. Daniel's adeptness with the tool had come as a surprise. But it eased much of the tension that had coiled within her over the past weeks.

Despite all the work that remained to be done, she and Daniel had made incredible strides. The plot for the barn was cleared and ready. And thanks to her husband's quick learning, two logs were already in place. Planting was moving right along. In contrast to the hopelessness that had gripped her after her father's death, hope and joy stirred in her soul.

Keturah placed her hand on Daniel's arm. His muscle corded as he pushed the plane forward, then relaxed when he stopped. He lifted a smile for her, despite his labored breathing. "Come, take a break," she urged.

Daniel leaned across the beam and kissed her on the cheek. "I need to finish this."

Keturah gave him a soft smile. "Nay. Ye need to take a break. We both need sustenance, an' I have a hankerin' for fish for supper. Why dinnae we go a'fishin'?" Not only would the fresh fish be a pleasant change in their meals, but the laid-back task would allow their sore muscles time to rest.

Daniel's expression hovered between a grimace and a grin. "As long as you do not mind teaching me how."

An unintended sigh escaped Keturah before she pushed the smile back onto her face. "Aye. I will show ye all ye need to know. Then we can fish alongside one another." Though it dimmed the appeal of her idea, it was not Daniel's fault that he did not know what he did not know. After all, they had been raised in completely different environments. And just as she had learned and adapted over the years, surely, he would do the same.

# CHAPTER 7

*June 1, 1782*

Keturah cringed as she trekked down to the bank of the Green River. If Scamper did not scare the fish away, Daniel would. The two crashed through the undergrowth like an unruly pair of wild pigs. With a shake of her head, she stepped from the trees, out onto the stone-strewn shore. Though the tan rocks clinked together with every step, her noise still did not rival that of her companions.

Stopping at the edge of the water where a branch reached out and covered them with shade, Keturah settled their supplies on the ground beside a driftwood log. Then she turned and scooped water into the empty wooden bucket she had brought for the spoils of their labor.

"What is that for?" Daniel drew near and peered into the empty bucket.

With lips pursed, Keturah glanced in his direction. "To put the fish in after we catch them. 'Tis best to keep them wet an' alive until it is time to clean them."

"Clean them?"

Keturah stifled a groan. She would much rather settle in for a quiet afternoon, but Daniel could not learn without her sharing her knowledge. And his voice was so innocent and curious. It was endearing in its own way. "Removin' the bones an' scales. Cuttin' the meat out." She imitated the motions with her hands before she sat, using the log as a low bench.

Daniel came over to join her, the driftwood sinking lower with his weight.

Scamper crowded close, sniffing at the supplies in her basket.

"Here." She handed Daniel one of the poles she and her father had made from rivercane harvested on that very bank. He appraised the pole with interest, scanning it up and down. Keturah tapped him on the shoulder, then showed him how to unwind the waxed linen thread wrapped around its length without undoing the portion tied on in case a fish broke the pole. She had no desire to make repairs should Daniel disrupt it.

Once that task was complete, Keturah dug a couple of worms out of a second bucket and handed one to Daniel. With a straight face, he took it from her.

Digging them up from beneath rocks, he had not been quite so stoic. When she explained what they were doing, his eyes had increased to the size of saucers. But, he had delved right into the task, even with a grimace firmly in place. Now, he watched her for what to do next. Without hesitation, she pieced the worm with the hand-forged hook and pushed the hook along its length. Daniel did not protest, but his Adam's apple bobbed before he did the same.

"What now?"

Keturah smiled. "Now, ye toss it out there an' wait."

"How do you know if you catch one?"

She chuckled and gave him a nod. "Ye'll know." Keturah stretched her legs out and crossed one ankle over the other. "Did ye really never go fishin' growin' up?"

Daniel shook his head, and his dark hair flopped handsomely over his forehead, long since fallen from the perfectly combed state of that morning. "We lived near the city, and the household staff purchased and prepared the food." He shrugged a shoulder. "There was simply never a need."

"Hmm." Keturah tilted her face as she considered that sort of life. Before her family came west, they lived on the outskirts of town with land enough to grow a garden while her father worked as a fisherman on the Potomac River. Never had she lived in a home with more than a single room. Meanwhile, her husband had grown up in one with hired help.

But what did that home look like? Besides being devoid of a loving family? Keturah frowned. Since their marriage, Daniel had worked tirelessly by her side without complaint. Each night, they were bone weary with little energy left for conversation. Over two weeks had passed, and she still knew so little of her husband. Maybe it was time to remedy that.

~

Keturah hummed as she settled their plates on the table, the tantalizing smell of breaded catfish filling her senses. Both of the plates overflowed with fish and potatoes, and a third plate sat to the side, heaped with more fish. Not only had their fishing expedition been exceptionally prosperous, but Daniel had proven adept at cleaning and fileting the fish. The man surprised her at every turn.

His deep, comforting voice drifted to her from where he sat in the rocking chair by the hearth reading from his Bible, and a smile tugged at her lips. "'Herein is love, not that we have loved God, but that he loved us, and sent his son to be the propitiation for our sins. Beloved, if God so loved us, we ought also love one another. No man hath seen God at any time. If we love one another, God dwelleth in us, and his love is perfected within us.'"

As Daniel's words washed over Keturah, she stopped in her tracks and turned toward him. Did he choose that verse intentionally? Nay, he had begun at the beginning of 1 John and continued to rock and read even now, Scamper stretched out on the floor beside him.

But still, the verse tugged at Keturah's spirit. How guilty she was of not living out those words. When God had showed such love in the offering of His own Son, she had failed to extend more than an ounce of affection to her husband. To the man who she had vowed before God to cherish. Keturah swallowed as she considered how critical she had been of her husband over the last couple of weeks. Even when her words showed grace, how often had her thoughts been critical and judgmental? Guilt squeezed at her heart.

Going forward, she must strive to do better. Just because Daniel was not what Keturah had imagined in a husband did not mean that he did not deserve her love. Not only had she made her marriage vows before God, but she had given Daniel her word. It was time she lived up to that. To make every effort to show him love and compassion.

As Keturah approached the rocker, Daniel closed the Bible, ceased his rocking, and began to hum a melody she had never heard. The sound was rich and wonderful, washing over her like a warm blanket on a cold winter day. Stopping a couple of steps away, she closed her eyes and relished its comforting touch, allowing it to envelop her and work its way into her soul.

Eventually, the humming turned to words, and a smile stretched Keturah's lips as she crept up behind the rocker. Her husband had a mesmerizing singing voice. Careful not to disturb him, she leaned ever so lightly against the chair-back and placed her cheek on her hand as she listened to the conclusion of the song. The dying embers of the fire they had used to fry the fish flickered in the hearth, making the moment all the more enchanting.

All too soon, the tune ended, and Daniel turned to peer up at her with a broad, affectionate smile that let her know he had known she was there all along.

Heat crept up her neck. "What was that?"

"A song Nanny used to sing me as a child." His gaze grew wistful.

Keturah's heart ached as she recalled the little he had shared regarding his upbringing while they were at Skaggs's Station. She reached down to his shoulder, her hand resting on the smooth silk of the waistcoat he still insisted upon wearing each night once he washed up for supper. A sudden longing to know her husband better opened deep within her. "Will ye share more about yer childhood with me while we eat?"

Daniel took her hand into his, his thumb drawing circles on the smooth skin on the back, as he smiled up at her. "I would be glad to. As long as you share more about yourself as well."

Keturah groaned but returned his grin. "I suppose."

"Good." Daniel gave a hearty chuckle as he stood

and led her over to the table where their plates waited, Scamper right on their heels. The pup had taken to hiding beneath the table during meals in hopes that he would come into some scraps. Keturah and Daniel settled into their places beside one another and held a hand as they bowed their heads for grace. "Thank You, Lord, for the bounty before us and the family around us. May You bless this food to the nourishment of our bodies and fill our home with love. We look to You, Lord, in everything and pray that You lead us on our journey. Amen."

Keturah could not help the blush that crept into her cheeks as she withdrew her hand and took up her fork. She cleared her throat. "Tell me more about yer nanny," she requested before she stuffed her mouth with catfish.

A melancholy smile passed over Daniel's face. "She never had children, so she treated me as her own, caring for me in a way that no one else ever did. She saw to my schooling, read stories to me. She is where I gained my love of learning and reading." Daniel motioned to where the leather case full of books sat beside the wardrobe, waiting for the shelf to be built to house them.

Though Father had never thought much of reading, Keturah looked forward to diving into some of the volumes come winter when there would be more time for such luxuries. "She sounds like a wonderful woman. What was her name?"

"Clarice. Of course, she was always *Nanny* to me. But I always thought she had a beautiful name."

Keturah nodded. "'Tis a bonny name."

Daniel shot her a wide grin that made her insides swirl. "As is yours. From the Bible, correct?"

This drew a smile from Keturah. "Aye. Me mither chose it." Her lips dipped downward then. "Father would never call me Keturah, though. He called me Ceit. What he considered a good Scottish name."

"I am sorry to hear that. Your name is as gorgeous and unique as you are." Daniel's warm gaze swept over her before he pushed a curl behind her ear. Those golden-brown eyes of his seemed to pierce right into her soul.

She shook her head. "Me father never thought much of me. Of women, in general. When I was young, I thought I could earn his love. I worked hard, became as good a shot as him an' me brother." Keturah leaned toward Daniel. "Maybe even better, though neither would ever admit it. I thought if I were good enough, he would finally take me on a hunt as he did with me brother. He never did ask, so one mornin', I hid in bed, all dressed an' prepared while they readied for their hunt. As soon as they stepped outside, I went after them. But the moment I opened the door, me father turned on me. I was not welcome an' never would be. I was a girl, an' all I would ever be good for was tendin' house an' raisin' bairns. Of course, that dinnae stop him from usin' me to do a woman's *an'* a man's work when we made it here to Kentucky an' 'twas only the two of us."

"Oh, Keturah." Daniel's voice was soft and gentle as he placed a hand upon her forearm. "You said at Skaggs's Station that you knew what it was like to be blamed for your mother's death. Was it your father who blamed you?"

Keturah's stomach dropped, and she swallowed. Would Daniel understand? Surely, he would. "Aye. In tryin' to gain his respect an' acceptance, I encouraged a dangerous river crossin' that only he wanted to pursue. Me mither an' me brother both died that day. Me mither was swept away by the current, an' me brother went back in to try an' save her." A single tear slipped down her cheek. "I blamed meself as well until I met me friend Margaret an' she helped me realize 'twas not me fault."

Given how Daniel's past aligned with hers, perhaps he would hear the relief in her voice and realize that he, too, could be free of the shackles of guilt. But there was still so much pain in his eyes when he met her gaze. So yes, he truly understood the sting of blame and rejection. Of never being good enough.

"It is sometimes difficult to remember the truths of reality when you are being fed a lie. When loneliness seems your only companion." Daniel's mouth pulled into a thin line.

Keturah's heart seemed to twist within her chest.

She scanned her husband's face, taking in every ounce of hurt and pain before she ran her fingers along his jawline. "Now ye dinnae have to be so lonely."

Daniel slid closer to her on the bench seat. His lips tugged upward as he caressed her cheek with his thumb. Keturah closed her eyes and leaned into his touch. Maybe a husband such as Daniel would be more of a blessing than she ever could have imagined. Not only was his touch so loving and tender that it sent sweet ripples through her middle, but now she had a companion and confidant. One who seemed to fill a broken place inside her. A place that had been lonelier than she ever realized.

But now, as she nestled into her husband's embrace and accepted his touch, a craving awakened within her soul. A craving for the closeness and understanding he offered. Lifting her eyes to Daniel's affectionate gaze, she moved closer and placed her hand upon the soft, smooth-shaven skin along his jaw. He closed his eyes for only a moment, and when he opened them, they were filled with the same heat and longing she felt within.

His lips came down to meet hers. They melded so perfectly together, it was as though they had been made for each other. Was it possible God had created this man for her and she for him? After all, what were the chances that two people whose stories coincided so well would find one another?

As she leaned into the sensation of healing that came with Daniel's kiss, she felt more whole than she had in months, if not years. The homestead was far from her mind as hope for her marriage and her future with her husband bloomed inside her chest. Could there be more to her life than she had ever imagined?

# CHAPTER 8

*June 30, 1782*

Daniel grunted as he and Iain lifted the twelve-foot timber into place. Sweat slid down his chest below where his linen shirt hung open at his neck, and he gave the log a final shove to lock it into the one beneath it. Standing back to admire his work, he rubbed the back of his arm over his brow.

"She's a'comin' together." Iain nodded, his own sleeves rolled above his elbows.

"Thanks to your help." Daniel clapped his comrade on the shoulder. If it were not for Keturah's friend, Margaret, and her husband coming for an extended visit, the barn would not be more than halfway complete as it was now.

"We are glad to be here." The corners of Iain's blue eyes crinkled as he gave Daniel a weary smile. Though the man's help had been invaluable, the couple's actual reason for visiting was to share their joyous news—Margaret was expecting. A tiny addition to the Donegal family was due to arrive in early winter.

"And we are glad to have you." Daniel returned the man's smile, then nodded to where the sun hung low over the tree line. "Though I suppose we should wash up before the women call us in for supper."

"Aye. That we should." Iain ran a hand through his hair, causing it to stick out at all angles.

Better not to know how disheveled and unpresentable Daniel himself appeared. 'Twas an aspect of frontier life he had come to accept. There was no sense in worrying over one's presentation when toiling on your own property—or among friends who understood the same. Still, he would wash up and don his waistcoat before they dined with their guests. He had not missed the appreciative glances Keturah sent his way when he wore it.

Iain followed Daniel into the house, where Scamper greeted them with a chorus of happy barks. Daniel bent to ruffle the growing pup's ears while Iain swooped in to give his wife a kiss. Margaret did not seem to mind that her husband was covered in sweat and grime. Instead, love reflected in her warm gaze as she captured Iain's hand and rubbed the back of it affectionately.

Daniel's gaze lifted to where Keturah was setting the table with plates. Her green eyes caught his and she stilled, lips parted. The corners of his mouth lifted as she ducked back to her task and a flush colored her cheeks.

Over the past month, they had discovered the wonders of intimacy a marriage held. But Keturah appeared a bit insecure in expressing her affections since the arrival of their houseguests. He could not blame her. It was all so new. Unlike the seasoned couple whose toddler played on the floor near the hearth, they were still discovering what love meant. In fact, they had yet to share those exact words with one another. But tonight, Daniel planned to remedy that. After supper, he would give Keturah the ring and declare his love for her.

~

"Let me finish that, an' ye can go spend some time with yer husband." Margaret placed a hand on Keturah's arm and gave her a knowing smile. Keturah blushed for what seemed the millionth time since her friend's arrival, but managed to purse her lips and raise her brow.

"Ye dinnae need to be washin' these dishes for me."

Margaret chuckled. "Ye know good an' well a woman cannae stop washin' dishes simply 'cause she is with child. An' after all, that is the last one." Her friend's lips twisted into a smirk as she pointed to the plate in Keturah's hand.

Keturah groaned and relinquished the dish into

Margaret's care. She had become so caught up attempting to act normal in front of their guests that she had done the complete opposite.

"Ye dinnae need to be afraid to show yer love in front of us," Margaret added.

She snuck a glance to where Daniel sat on the floor with Iain and his son. Daniel marched little wooden animals across the floor while Alexander imitated their sounds. Her hand went to her stomach. Would their own union be blessed with children soon? Her heart warmed at the idea, and for the first time in a while, prayer came easily. *Lord, thank Ye for blessin' me with such a man, an' please continue to bless our marriage.*

Daniel looked up at her and smiled as though he read her thoughts. Then he excused himself and came to her, offering his arm. "Would you care for a moonlit stroll, m'lady?"

Warmth and affection blossomed in her chest. "Gladly." She grinned as she accepted his arm and allowed him to usher her from the room. Oh, how this man made her smile.

Out into the refreshing night air he led her. Above them, tiny stars blinked out from an inky black sky. Slowly and silently, they strolled over the dew-dampened ground. The night could not be more perfect. Good friends, mild weather, and a man who loved her.

Keturah's breath hitched, and she slid a glance up at Daniel. He did love her, right? The kindness, humor, and physical affection that he showered upon her spoke of love, and yet, the word had never slipped from his lips. Keturah frowned. She knew so little of men and their minds.

Daniel's brows knit together as he turned to face her, pulling her into his arms. "What is concerning you, my love?"

Keturah's lips parted and time stilled as they both registered his endearment. She searched Daniel's wide eyes. Had he meant to say it?

His expression softened, and his mouth eased into a smile. He pulled her closer into him. "It is about time that you knew that I do indeed love you." He brought his hand up and gently caressed her cheek with his thumb.

Keturah closed her eyes and leaned into his touch. "I love ye too." The whispered words slipped effortlessly from her mouth.

"Oh, Keturah, my love." Daniel's lips met hers in a gentle yet sensual kiss that caused her insides to swirl and had her pressing up onto her toes, into him. She had never imagined marriage could be like this.

Daniel pulled away all too soon. He reached into the pocket of his dashing black waistcoat and withdrew a small pouch. Keturah leaned forward as he pulled a ring from its depths. Daniel held it up for her in the moonlight. She sucked in a breath. It was exquisite, like none she had ever seen. Multiple stones in the middle made the appearance of a flower, nestled between two intricate roses. "It was Nanny's mother's. She gave it to me before I left." He took her left hand and slipped the ring onto her finger. "And now, it is yours. I should have given it to you the moment we were married, but I wanted it to be a symbol of our love, not just of a convenience marriage."

Keturah leaned into Daniel, her hands spread on his chest. "'Tis perfect." She rewarded him with a long kiss, one hand venturing into the hair at his nape. Would this man ever cease to amaze her?

∼

*July 28, 1782*

Daniel stifled a yawn as he shuffled through the open doorway of the almost-complete barn to the pen where the pig was kept. He carried the remnants of breakfast in the slop bucket, to be dumped in with the hungry animal. However, as Daniel neared the stall door, he stopped in his tracks.

"Gilly?" He repeated the name he had heard Keturah use for the pig as he approached and peered into the dark, damp stall. His nose curled at the foul smell, but it was not the cause for the concern that gripped his middle. When no movement met his eyes or ears, he stepped inside and quickly swept his gaze over the small room to ensure he had not missed the animal. Nothing but mud. A groan slipped from his chest.

Their pig, which was well past due for giving birth, was gone. And it was his fault. It had to be. He had been the last one to take the slop out to her the night before. He checked the bar on the gate. Had he not properly shut the door? He flattened his mouth and ran a hand through his hair. It was the only explanation. And one he did not look forward to sharing with his wife.

Perhaps it would be better if he attempted to locate the animal and return her home before alerting Keturah to his latest failure. A sigh slipped from Daniel as he considered raising her ire. He and Keturah had grown quite close as he proved himself adequate in the construction of the barn. He did not wish to harm the relationship that had formed between them, still so new and fragile. And that meant finding the pig before his wife knew she was missing.

Daniel set the slop bucket in front of the stall and stepped outside, glancing around. "Gilly! Here, girl," he called and paused to listen. He banked around the edge of the building, calling for the animal before he moved onto the garden and cornfield. Over and over he called, but nowhere did he spy the large pink-and-black pig. He gazed across the valley meadow with his hands on his hips. The sun warmed his back. How far could such a rotund animal with such stubby legs have gone in only one night?

Moving into the shade of the tree line, he cupped his hands around his mouth and called up the hill behind the cabin. But only the breeze ruffled the green plants of the underbrush.

"What is all that hollerin' about?"

Daniel stopped in his tracks at the sound of Keturah's voice. Grimacing, he turned on his heel to face the wrath of his wife. She stood beside the cabin, drying her hands on her apron. A pucker had formed between her eyebrows, and her lips were drawn.

"The pig has escaped."

Keturah's eyes widened, and her hands froze in her apron. "What?"

"The pig. I must not have latched the stall door properly, for it was open when I came out here, and she seems to be missing." He gestured wide with his arms.

Keturah took a step toward him. "Daniel! She is overdue with them piglets! I had her in the barn for a reason!"

Daniel's mouth firmed. As soon as the walls were in place, he and Keturah had moved the pig, which normally roamed freely, into the barn for monitoring. Though it was an honest mistake, he had failed his wife. "I understand that. And I am trying to find her." He did not mean for his voice to come out as tight as it did, and it earned a glare from Keturah.

Would he ever stop disappointing people?

## CHAPTER 9

How could Daniel have been so careless? Keturah's blood boiled as she stared at the open stall door, her hands on her hips. Her foot tapped as she surveyed the ground in search of clues as to where the pig had gone. She was to be a first-time mother and should have already delivered. Undue stress could be disastrous. Not to mention, the much-needed income that would be lost if she and her piglets were never found.

Keturah closed her eyes and took a deep breath. She would not think about that yet.

But as she stared at the ground, her mouth twisted. Not only had her husband left the gate open for the pig to escape, but he had trampled all over the tracks leading from the stall. Keturah did her best to follow them, but with the weather having been dry, the gilt had left little trace. Still, she was positive she was following in the correct direction. That was, until she reached the grass outside the barn. As she looked up, her heart plummeted. The animal could have gone anywhere from here.

Still, she forged ahead. "This way," she called to Daniel, who stood in the barn doorway, and waved her hand.

Keturah did not wait around to see if he followed. Instead, she marched across the grass, still wet with the morning dew, and into the woods. "Gilly!" She called out the nickname she had given the animal. Her gaze alternated between scanning the underbrush for movement and searching the ground before her for some clue as to if the animal had been through there. When she spied a broken twig, she knelt to examine it further. Near it were other sticks that showed evidence of a rooting animal.

"Gilly!"

At her husband's booming voice behind her, Keturah ducked. She turned and glared up at him, but without glancing her way, he marched past, deeper into the woods. She groaned as she rose from the ground and pursued him. Daniel would be more hassle than help, for she had to ensure she did not lose him in the woods as well. "Wait," she called after him.

"Should we not spread out to cover more ground?" Daniel's brow furrowed and the corners of his mouth pulled down as he looked from her out into the forest.

"No, we dinnae need to be separated. If we do find

her, it will take the both of us to return her to the barn." Though she spoke the truth, she said it only to persuade her husband to stick close. While there was no good way to move a pig, Keturah had handled the animal on her own before. Thankfully, the words must have done their trick, for Daniel waited where he stood before following her as she delved deeper into the woods.

Keturah scoured the ground for hoof prints and other signs. The area they wove through was one the animal had frequented before she was moved to the barn. In fact, they were nearing the small clearing where Keturah and her father had occasionally put out corn to entice the pig into remaining close to home. Hope bubbled within her.

But as Keturah broke through the trees, the clearing was empty save for a few rays of sunlight that pierced the canopy of trees. A grumble ripped from her chest as her hands clenched at her sides.

Daniel huffed up behind her. "Did you lose the trail?"

Keturah gritted her teeth to keep from saying something she would regret. No, she had lost nothing, quite unlike him. But then again, how could she admit she had no inkling where the animal was either?

Ignoring her husband, she marched into the clearing. There, she gave the long, loud whooping noise her father had used to call the pig. Her cheeks heated at the embarrassing sound, but it needed to be done. Much to her dismay, the only answer was the rustle of the breeze through the oak leaves and the squawk of a blue jay. Mouth set firmly, Keturah looked around. Where would the animal have gone?

Closing her eyes, she stopped to consider what the pig would eat on her own. Insects, mushrooms, worms... most of which were more abundant closer to the spring. Turning to her right, Keturah struck off once more, with Daniel on her heels. They maneuvered over roots and under tree limbs. A chipmunk darted away as she pushed a thick grapevine out of her way and held it for Daniel to move past. Instead, he reached up and held the dry brown vegetation and motioned for her to continue on.

Keturah ducked under and picked her way past some poison oak clinging to the base of the tree the vine hung from. Then she crossed over a patch of dark-green moss, a clear indication they were moving in the right direction. This was the kind of area where the gilt could find a plethora of food. If only they could find her...

Keturah skirted around a broad pine tree and stopped in her tracks. There stood the pig, so engrossed in her rooting that she paid them no heed. "Gilly," she cried as relief flooded through her. Without thinking, she tromped toward the animal and immediately regretted the action. Her loud footsteps drew the gilt's head from the ground, and grunting, she darted away.

"Stop her!" Keturah threw the instruction toward

her husband as she pointed after the pig, even though he was no closer to the animal than she was. But a mad dash ensued as they both ran in her direction.

Daniel gained on the pig first, but when he dove toward the animal, he ended up with a face full of fern. Keturah plowed right on past him. Sputtering, he lifted himself from the ground as Keturah hiked her petticoats above her ankles so she could pursue the gilt over the uneven terrain without snagging them on everything in sight.

The pig headed east along the creek, grunts emanating from her rotund body and her head bobbing as she went. It was surprising how quickly her short little legs could carry her as she pushed past shrubs and saplings along the creek bank. Stones clattered under Keturah's feet and toppled into the shallow water as she kicked them in her haste to catch up. A thorn bush grabbed her underskirt, and she grimaced at the sound of ripping fabric. She had no time to stop and survey the damage, though. The garment could be mended after the pig was safely back in the barn.

Finally, Keturah gained on the gilt. She reached out, but the animal darted around a large rock that protruded from the ground. In an attempt to stop short of the obstacle, Keturah stumbled and fell. She groaned as a root dug into her back.

Daniel's concerned face appeared above her. As he started to kneel and reach out to her, she waved him away.

"I am fine! Get the pig!" Keturah worked herself into a kneeling position and swiped the curls from her face that had escaped their pins. When she followed after Gilly and Daniel, she breathed a sigh of relief. The pig now angled toward the homestead. "Keep her going in that direction," she called after her husband. They could worry about wrangling the beast once she was near home.

Keturah thought she caught a nod as Daniel leapt over a small, downed tree the pig darted under. She followed as quickly as her cumbersome garments would allow. Sweat slipped down her temples and beaded between her breasts as she continued the chase. Again, how could such an awkward animal be so agile and quick? Keturah shook her head as she dashed through the trees.

But she and Daniel both came skidding to a halt when the pig plowed straight into a thicket of bushes so dense that they could not follow. Keturah let out a growl of frustration as Daniel ran a hand through his dark, damp hair.

His chest heaved with exertion. "We will have to go around."

Keturah nodded, and they darted around the bush in time to see the gilt burst through the leaves on the other side. Her thick hide sported several cuts that made Keturah wince. She needed Gilly home, safe and sound. She had babies to bring into the world, and hopefully soon. Concern wound its way through her middle at the thought. All this running could not be good for Gilly or the piglets, could it?

Finally, they broke through the trees and into the valley where the homestead sat. As the pig neared the barn, she slowed to a trot. And then a walk. For as surprisingly fast as her short legs had carried her before, now their pace was painstakingly slow. It was as though she had figured out their plan and had no interest in returning to her stall.

Keturah slowed and kept her distance for fear of spooking her again.

Daniel walked ahead. "Come on, girl. Come get the slop I have for you." He motioned to the animal as though she understood what he said. Gilly stopped completely and gave a snort.

Keturah groaned before she sent a withering glance toward her husband.

He paid her no heed and continued on, still calling to the animal that snorted and pretended to inspect the ground.

When the animal did not budge, Keturah moved forward and shoved on her from behind. "Come on, this a way." Her own grunt slipped out as she pushed with all her might, her shoulder pressed against the animal's rump, to no avail.

Suddenly, Daniel was behind her with a tree branch in hand. "Can you block the far side of the barn?"

Keturah looked him over and raised an eyebrow. "What do ye plan to do?"

He gave her a pointed look, his brown eyes sharp and his mouth turned down at the corners. "I am going to try to herd her."

Keturah's hands balled into fists as tension sizzled between them. Who was he to think the pig would respond to him over her? Not only did he know not a thing about pigs, but this entire ordeal was his fault. Still, they had little other choice, given the circumstances.

After turning on her heel, she trudged over to the barn aisle. Opening the stall door wide, she placed herself in the opening between the stall and the other side of the barn. Daniel whipped the branch up and down behind the pig, and Gilly took off again, straight toward Keturah. She bent, widening her stance, and waved her arms in the air. Then, as she yelled at the top of her lungs, she witnessed a miracle. The pig ran right into her stall without a moment's hesitation. Keturah paused only a second before she leapt forward and slammed the gate behind her. After ensuring it was properly locked, she turned and leaned against the stall door.

Closing her eyes, she took a deep breath. Gilly was safely back in her stall. Thanks to Daniel. Keturah's middle tightened. An apology was in order. But when she opened her eyes, her husband was nowhere in sight.

~

*A*nger rippled through Daniel as he stalked back to the house. Yes, the pig's escape was his fault—there was no denying it. But the look his wife had given him when he stated he would herd the animal back to her stall...as though he was an imbecile, incapable of even the simplest task. He had seen such utter disdain before. Had dealt with it within his own home before. But thus far, it had seemed life could be different with Keturah.

Daniel marched across the porch and through the cabin door, only to stop in his tracks. His shoulders sagged as he entered the dimly lit interior. He trudged over to the rocking chair beside the hearth, the fight gone from him. Scamper lifted his head and gave him a tongue-out, tail-wagging grin. The greeting caused the corners of Daniel's mouth to lift a little.

He settled in the rocker, and Scamper jumped up, placing his paws on his knees. My, how the pup had already grown. "Can you imagine what would have happened if you had been a part of the chase?" Daniel chuckled. How comical it would have been had the dog been allowed to help chase the pig. They likely never would have returned the animal home.

Light poured into the room as Keturah came inside. Her curls were all askew, and pieces of leaves clung to her hair while her ripped petticoat dragged along the cabin floor, peeking out from under her top layers. Her expression was somber as she approached, and he braced himself for what she might say.

"Thank you." The words were barely audible.

Daniel blinked up at Keturah. "For what?"

"For gettin' Gilly back in her stall."

"Oh." Daniel nodded, his gaze dropping to the brown-eyed puppy face that stared up at him. While he appreciated the thanks, the nature of it chafed. Did it have to seem so difficult for her to express gratitude? Especially after she had displayed such contempt earlier. "'Twas the least I could do."

Keturah attempted a smile, but her lips wobbled and her eyes glistened. Then she walked away and began to gather the flour and supplies for baking bread.

Daniel's brow furrowed. What an odd encounter with his normally spirited wife. Did a simple apology truly drain so much from her?

## CHAPTER 10

*August 19, 1782*

Keturah groaned and dropped her sewing onto her lap. Her seam was crooked...again. She leaned her head back against the rocking chair as tears formed in her eyes. Why could she not get this right? She may not have the talent of a seamstress, but her sewing skills were perfectly adequate, and this was nowhere near her first time forming her own clothing. But for some reason, she could not seem to make the fabric of her father's tartan work with her. She had ripped the seams out and redone them more times that she could count. And still, it was not ready to be worn over her petticoats.

She blew out an exasperated breath. Perhaps she should visit Daniel and Scamper outside. Her husband had finally found an opportunity to work on their bookcase, and though Keturah attempted to be productive as well, her efforts had failed. Better to breathe in the fresh air than to wallow. Yet, wallowing was all she felt she had energy for. It was quite unlike her. So she rose and went to the door, poking her head outside.

At least the heat was not as stifling as it was indoors. Keturah stepped out onto the porch and fanned her face with her hand. Maybe that had been her first mistake, attempting to work the wool in the dead of summer. 'Twas no wonder she could not focus.

Still, she felt…off. Her emotions had been all over the place for nearly a month, it seemed. Keturah left the porch and moved over to Daniel's side. His dark hair poked in every which direction as he hammered in the last nail on the bottom shelf. When he straightened, Keturah ran her hand through his sweat-dampened locks to restore order. "I should draw ye a bath before I prepare the meal."

Daniel took her hands into his. "No. There is no need for you to trouble yourself on my behalf. The creek shall be more refreshing on a day such as this, anyway."

Tears formed in Keturah's eyes as she peered up at her sweet husband.

His brow puckered. "Keturah, what is wrong, my love?" He drew her into him as she shook her head.

"I dinnae know. I suppose 'tis nice to have someone

consider me." She shrugged a shoulder. "To lighten me load rather than add to it. Father always needed me to do somethin' to make *his* life easier. Always."

Daniel hugged her tightly. "No more, my dear. No more."

Keturah squeezed her eyes shut and took solace in her husband's comforting embrace. *Thank Ye, Lord.* Though she had doubted God's presence in her life, His hand in it was now evident. Daniel had proved to be anything but the naïve, bumbling dandy she once worried he was. Instead, he completed her and provided the support she had never before received.

Still, that did not explain her sudden propensity for tears.

∼

*August 26, 1782*

Keturah sighed contentedly as she stirred the stew in a pot over an outdoor fire. The day was gorgeous, with warm sunshine overhead and a gentle breeze rustling through the valley. Scamper laid stretched across the grass several yards away, positioned between her and Daniel, basking in the glory.

Daniel sat propped against a tall red maple, whittling a stick. Well, it was more than a stick. The piece of wood he had chosen to work with was nearly as big around as her wrist. Her lips pulled into a smile, and she gave the food another stir to keep the bits of potato and carrot from sticking to the bottom. Perhaps her husband would be talented at woodcarving, considering how he had taken to construction with ease.

She glanced at his profile again, at the sweep of his dark hair over his forehead. His lips pressed together as he concentrated on the task at hand, chipping away at the wood with a knife. What would he create? Would it be something she could sit upon the mantel as a token of his talent and a reminder of the man who had stolen her heart?

Scamper barked suddenly, scaring her from her thoughts. When she turned, he was snapping at a butterfly as it flew by. He jumped to his feet and gave chase. Keturah shook her head even though her lips stretched in a smile. She did have to agree with her husband that the pup had grown much in the short months they had been married. No longer truly a pup, he was long and lean. Though whether he would ever be a hunting dog was still debatable. Much like his owner, he was too easily distracted.

A giggle passed through her lips, and she pressed a hand to her mouth. Keturah could not help the joy that overflowed, though. For she had finally discovered the reason for her moodiness—she was with child.

"Keturah."

Keturah lifted her head, her brows bunching as her husband's tentative voice drifted to her from his place beside the tree. Dread coiled in the pit of her stomach at the particular timbre. Slowly, she turned toward him.

Some of the tension released from her shoulders at the sight of the apologetic grin on Daniel's face. But he seemed to be fighting a grimace, and he curled his right hand against his chest, cradled in his left one.

Keturah made for her husband. "What happened?"

Daniel winced. "I, um...there was an accident."

Her heart picked up its pace. "What kind of accident?"

Daniel finally held up his hand. Bright red blood dripped in a steady stream from a large deep gash in the back of his hand.

Keturah's eyes widened as she sucked in a breath. "How on earth...?" She dropped to her knees beside him, examining the wound. "Come to the house," she ordered, immediately rising again.

Daniel followed obediently and without a word as she marched across the clearing and into the cabin.

Inside, Keturah pointed to the bench beside the table. "Sit."

She went to fetch the jug of water and basin from beside the bed, then moved alongside her husband. Ignoring the trail of blood that led across the room, she placed Daniel's injured hand in the basin and poured water over it, washing free any debris that might be in the gash. Keturah leaned closer to the cut, but blood still seeped so quickly from the opening that she could not see if it had been thoroughly cleaned. And the wound would need to be pristine before the flesh was stitched back together. Keturah pursed her lips and went to the cabinet where her father had kept the dreaded drink that made his moods worse.

"This will hurt," she warned Daniel as she returned.

He nodded his assent, his face tight with pain. When she poured the amber-colored liquid over the cut, her husband hissed out a breath.

As the wound filled again with blood, Keturah groaned. Glancing about the room, she racked her brain for some way to stop the bleeding. Salt.

Dashing back over to the hutch along the wall, she lifted the canister of salt from the shelf and whisked it over to where Daniel sat. Keturah swallowed at how pale his face had become. How could one wound bleed so much? Should it not have stopped by now? Hoping her face did not reveal her concern, she settled onto the bench next to Daniel and scooped salt into the gash on the back of his right hand.

"Ahh." Instinctively, he tried to jerk back as pain no doubt shot through his arm, but she held tight to his larger hand.

Once she had loaded it with salt, she retrieved a dish towel and wrapped it tightly around his hand. Then she pressed it to him for him to hug against his body. Her other hand did not leave his shoulder as her gaze went to his face. "That should staunch the bleedin'. Then I will clean it again an' stitch it up."

Daniel nodded, though his jaw remained set. Her heart beat wildly as she stared into his eyes. "All will be well," her husband whispered.

She forced a small smile to her lips. "Aye," she agreed, though concern caused her middle to tighten. A quick glance told her the towel had yet to soak through, but they were not out of the woods yet. Daniel's skin remained several shades paler than normal, evidence of the amount of blood already lost. The wound had yet to be stitched, and they could only pray that no infection set in. It was enough to bring tears to her eyes. But she blinked them back and busied herself with gathering her sewing basket so Daniel would not notice.

As she lifted the white-oak basket from the floor, Scamper's barking outside drew her notice. Dropping the basket off on the table near Daniel, she moved to the door, carefully avoiding the drops of blood marring the cabin floor. Swinging the door open, she gasped.

"What is it?" Daniel's voice came to her from the table.

"The stew," she called over her shoulder.

As she dashed out to where the pot hung over the crackling fire, the stew smoked and sputtered, displeased with her inattention. Keturah reached for the ladle that had been left inside the pot in her haste but quickly drew back. The metal had grown too hot to touch.

She lifted the towel draped over the stump she had been seated on earlier and used it to protect her hand as she attempted to save the stew. But as she stirred, the thick stew made an awful sucking sound. The bottom was surely burnt. Dropping the ladle, she moved her towel to the handle and lifted the pot from the hook to carefully move it inside. They would salvage all they could, and she would scrub the dish later. Once her husband was properly cared for and supper eaten.

Keturah placed the bubbling stew on top of a towel on the table and returned to Daniel's side. "How is it now?" She reached for his hand and started unwrapping. Her shoulders relaxed. The bleeding had stopped.

Daniel sought her gaze. "That is good."

Keturah sighed before she met Daniel's eyes again. "Now for the hard part."

Her husband forced a grin as he nodded. "I can handle it."

Keturah returned his nod as she searched his face. With the strength he had displayed since arriving at the homestead, she was confident that his words held truth. At least, she prayed so. Daniel had handled the blood well, but a needle dipping in and out of his flesh would be another story. She knew from experience. What would she do if he fainted? She forced the thought from her mind, focusing instead on threading the needle.

Keturah closed her eyes and sent a brief prayer heavenward. *Lord, please give me a steady hand.* "Ready?"

Daniel nodded.

Carefully, she cleaned the salt from the wound and poured her father's rum over it once more. The second cleaning caused a mild amount of bleeding, though nothing like before. Finally, Keturah put the needle to flesh, ignoring the deep groan from Daniel. She worked her way along the length of the gash, bringing the skin back together and sewing it in place. Blood seeped slowly out as she worked, and she used her free hand to wipe the wound clean with a cloth as she went. Daniel remained quiet but steadfast.

At last, the wound was stitched, and all bleeding ceased. Keturah could breathe again. When she looked her husband in the face, though, a wrinkle marred his brow. "Are ye well?"

The wrinkle disappeared, and he managed a smile for her, his complexion still far too pale. "Of course, I am. Thanks to you." Daniel leaned close and kissed her cheek.

Keturah smiled as warmth spread up from her neck. Following his lead, she ran her hand along the side of his face. "Yer sure?"

"Yes. It only hurts a little." Daniel lifted his wounded hand and inspected her sewing job. "Not as much as one would expect."

"Good. Let us get some stew in ye, an' then ye should rest." Keturah stood and went to the hutch for bowls.

A deep chuckle emanated from her husband. "I will

not argue with food or rest, but I really am well. You should not worry so much."

"But ye lost a great deal of blood." She ladled soup into a bowl and placed it before him, stopping to feel his forehead. "An' now we will need to watch ye for infection."

Daniel took her hand in his and squeezed it tightly. It did little to ease the heavy weight within her middle. What would she do if she and their bairn lost Daniel before the babe was even born?

~

"How exactly did ye cut yer hand?" Now that the initial danger had passed and they were filling their bellies with what Keturah salvaged of the stew, Daniel was not surprised she had questions. He glanced down at the puckered skin on the back of his right hand and frowned. The answer was another embarrassing addition to his failures.

"You know, I really am not sure. The knife was going up and away from me. I think it came back down on the back side." He tried to mimic the motion of his carving to see if the theory held any validity. Truly, how incompetent could he be as a man?

Keturah's lips twisted into a smile she clearly attempted to conceal. "How did ye manage that?"

Daniel shrugged, grateful for the grin on his wife's

face, even if it was at his expense. She bit her lip, then, and glanced at him as though hiding a secret. "What?" He drew the word out, suddenly curious.

"I wanted to tell ye at the perfect moment. But then ye hurt yerself..."

"Tell me what?"

"Yer to be a father." Keturah's hand went to her middle.

The breath left his lungs. "I...I what?" Could it be true?

His wife gave him an encouraging nod even as she chuckled. "I am with child."

Daniel let out a whoop before he leapt from the table. He pulled Keturah from her place on the bench and twirled her around. "We are going to be parents!"

"Daniel," Keturah cried as he continued to swirl her about. "Yer goin' to hurt yer hand!" But even as she protested, giggles emanated from his wife.

Daniel shook his head, but he slowed, drawing Keturah close in dance of the heart. "My hand will be just fine." Everything was to be much better than fine, and his heart was bursting with the joy of it. He paused. "How soon?"

"How soon?" Keturah's brow puckered.

"When will the baby be here?"

"Oh!" Her face registered recognition. "I would say in about seven months' time. So... March."

Daniel leaned in and gave his wife a deep, heartfelt kiss. This was really happening. He was to be a father.

After all the rejection and loneliness of his life. After the tentative start to this marriage of convenience. To think that love had grown between them, one that had culminated in new life. It was truly a miracle and gift from God.

# CHAPTER 11

*August 27, 1782*

Daniel stoked the remnants of the fire Keturah had used to prepare supper and glanced toward her. "Is there a chill in the air tonight?"

Her hands stilled on the green beans she was snapping, and her brow lowered. "Nay." In fact, summer had peaked with sweltering temperatures, and she had seriously considered cooking outside again that afternoon. The cabin had already been stuffy prior to the meal preparation, and to her, it had grown quite sweltering. The door was even propped open to allow in the tiniest of breezes.

That could only mean one thing. Keturah's stomach dropped. She dropped the green bean she was about to snap back in the bowl and quickly moved across the cabin to her husband's side. After she placed the back of her hand against his forehead, her heart stuttered a beat. "Yer warm."

When she moved her hand, Daniel replaced it with his own. His dark brows pulled together, and his mouth twisted before he gave a shrug. "I feel quite well."

Keturah frowned. "Ye need to lie down." She ushered him toward the bed. This could not be happening. Infection could not take hold of her husband. Once she had him settled in the bed, she asked to see his hand. She tilted it this way and that, drawing a candle closer in order to better assess it in the dim light of the cabin. "There is a wee bit of redness. Is it tender?" She ran her finger alongside the stitches, keeping her touch light.

Daniel smiled a smile that melted her insides and made her feel as though all would be well. "Not in the least bit."

Keturah pursed her lips and allowed her gaze to roam over his handsome face before she nodded. "Get some rest, an' I will check me mither's notebook to see if there is somethin' that can be done for infection. Just in case." She hesitated, then leaned over and pressed a kiss to her husband's warm lips. *Lord, please dinnae let it be our last. Please let him see the birth of our child.* She prayed silently as she blew out the candle and moved away from the bed.

Keturah went to retrieve the notebook in which her mother had written about the herbs and remedies she used, as well as her favorite recipes. Not that Ma had ever used the recipes for cooking. She had known them all by heart. Keturah smiled to herself, and a sudden ache stretched through her. Never again would she have the opportunity to learn from her mither about the things that were written in these pages. And never would her mither meet Daniel or their bairn. Their time together had been so short.

Her heart constricted. Would her time with her husband be even shorter? She glanced to where he slumbered. *Please, nay. Please, Lord, spare my husband an' keep the infection from him.* She sent the prayer heavenward.

Regret prickled up the back of her neck as she watched him. How much of their short marriage had she spent in judgement? She'd thought because he did not come from this land, this lifestyle, that he would prove incapable. Daniel was anything but inept, though, and love had begun to flourish between them in the past couple months.

Keturah sighed. She closed her eyes and squeezed them tight. Was it Daniel's lack of knowledge that had landed them here? Was she responsible for bringing him here, to his death? Nay, she could not believe such. This was a harsh, unforgiving land, and even a strong, knowledgeable man could be lost in the blink of an eye. Her father had been an example of that.

Keturah turned back to the notebook. Opening the cover, she stared down at her mother's handwriting. She had to find something helpful. Slowly, she scoured each page until the words blurred before her. She closed her eyes and leaned her head back to give them a rest. She could not stop until she found a remedy. Her husband needed her. And she him.

After a moment, Keturah resumed her search. She flipped the page and finally landed on a gem. Though she did not have the herb there on the homestead, she could find it. And while she had no desire to leave Daniel alone, it would be worth it if the plant would draw the infection from his hand as her mither had written it would.

Aye, she would go in search of the nettle...tomorrow. With a tiny bit of hope in her heart, Keturah leaned her head back again, her finger marking the page in the notebook. The fire crackled quietly behind her, her husband's breaths came slow and even, and Scamper let out a whimper in his sleep as his legs jerked, chasing after an imaginary rabbit. She smiled contentedly. Nights like this would be well worth it.

~

Where was she? Birds sang in the wee hours of morning, but Keturah's side of the bed remained undisturbed. Daniel snapped upright and glanced around. As his gaze settled on Keturah's sleeping form at the table, his heart started to slow its racing. Instead, a grin tipped up the side of his mouth. She must have fallen asleep reading her mother's notebook. He stood and went to her side. Sure enough, the book laid open under her head while her mouth hung agape.

Warmth spread through every inch of Daniel. His dear wife had stayed up until all hours of the night, all on his account. For the first time in his life, Daniel realized what it was to be truly loved. Even more than the physical intimacies of marriage or her spoken profession of love, this selfless act proved how deeply his wife cared.

He reached out and gently nudged her shoulder. "Keturah." He spoke her name quietly.

She jerked awake and looked both ways before her gaze landed on him. "Daniel." Her hand immediately went to his arm. She started to stand, but he settled on the bench next to her instead. "How are ye?" Her spring-green eyes searched his while a wrinkle formed in her brow and her mouth pinched.

"I am well." He smiled.

"Yer sure?" Keturah placed the back of her hand against his forehead. Then she took his hand in hers and examined the stitches as she had done the night before. This morning, there was not a trace of redness. To Daniel's surprise, though, Keturah frowned. "I may still find some of the nettle Ma wrote about. Just to be safe."

Daniel let out a chuckle as he turned his hand over and engulfed her smaller one in his, giving it a squeeze. "We can do whatever you wish, but I really am well." He met her eyes, imploring her to believe him.

Keturah searched his face. Tears swam in her eyes. "I just dinnae want to lose ye."

Daniel pulled her to him, nestling her against his chest. "Darling..." Her curls tickled his chin as he spoke, but he would not have it any other way. "Lord willing, I do not plan on going anywhere. We have a child to raise, after all."

Keturah tipped her head up to face him without leaving his embrace, her tears giving way to a smile. "That we do."

He wiped the moisture from her freckled cheek. All his life, Daniel had been searching. And right here it was, in the middle of nowhere in Kentucky. Love. Acceptance. Family. God had a plan all along. If only he had trusted Him.

∽

*September 4, 1782*

Keturah rolled over and stretched her arm out. While she still did not prefer to cuddle with Daniel while they slept, she had grown accustomed to reaching out to him each morning. But her hand found only empty covers, not the strong presence of her husband.

Keturah raised up onto her elbow and glanced

around. Daniel was nowhere to be found. Neither was Scamper. Her brow lowered. Quickly, she left the bed and dressed. Where could the two have gone? They never rose before her. Without bothering with her morning routine, she left her hair unkempt and face unwashed as she darted outside.

Stopping on the porch, she blinked as the bright light nearly blinded her. It was not early morning. No, judging from the location of the sun in the sky, it was only a couple of hours before noon. Her brow puckered even further. How could that have happened? She rarely slept past sunrise and did not feel unwell. In fact, she felt in better health than ever. Could the pregnancy be the cause for her tiredness?

Keturah walked across the yard to see if Daniel had started working without her. Her mouth dropped open as she took in the complete form of the barn. She darted to the other side and swept her gaze over the top. Every last inch of the roof had been covered in the wooden shingles they had finished preparing the day before. How had Daniel worked so quickly?

Daniel truly seemed to be coming into his own on the homestead. Though he remained inept with a gun, she could overlook that fact for his many redeeming qualities. Such as that he had proved to be quite handy when it came to manual labor. And had an eye for architecture. Without him, she was not sure how she would have ever completed the barn.

But here it stood, in all its glory. Would her father

have been proud? She frowned as the thought sliced through her. Keturah raised her chin. Nay, it did not matter whether he would have approved or not. She was proud of the work she and her husband had done alongside one another, and that was all that mattered. Where was that man, though?

Keturah glanced around. "Daniel," she called.

"In here," came the reply from within the depths of the barn. Keturah followed the sound and found him standing outside Gilly's stall.

"How is she?" She was apprehensive about asking the question considering the pig still had not delivered her piglets. Keturah had half come to expect that they would lose them all, the gilt and babes included. After all, her father had told her the animal would farrow out in the spring, and it was nearly fall. *Lord, please let him have been mistaken on that account.*

"Come see for yourself." Daniel's smile was broad as he invited her over.

She joined him and peered into the stall. A gasp flew from her lips. There, nestled beside Gilly, were ten little piglets, all rooting and nursing. Keturah found herself laughing and smiling so wide that her cheeks hurt as she watched the little ones. Here they were, standing under the newly completed barn, with all the piglets delivered safe and sound.

"Did all of them make it?" She turned to Daniel for confirmation.

He nodded as he gave her a gentle grin. "The best that I can tell."

Keturah breathed a sigh of relief. "Good."

She and Daniel stood watching the pigs for some time longer before he turned back to her. "You slept quite late. Is all well?"

Keturah's cheeks heated, and she peered up at Daniel through her lashes as she gave him a tentative smile. "I dinnae mean to."

"But you are feeling well?" Daniel looked at her pointedly, and his concern was heartening.

"Aye. I must have worn meself down a bit. Or the bairn is takin' me energy." She rubbed her middle, though it had yet to begin its expansion. Simply knowing a tiny life grew within was miraculous.

"Well, you should take a well-deserved break today, then. We should have a picnic lunch."

Keturah grimaced as she glanced out into the sunlight. The garden needed tending. "I dinnae…"

Before she could finish, Daniel held up a hand. "Whatever it is, it will keep. Come on, enjoy the day with me." As he held out his hand to her, he flashed her his winning smile—the one that had the power to melt her resolve even in the midst of a disagreement. She returned it with an impish grin of her own before placing her hand in his.

Warmth spread upward from her hand, and she knew their plans for the afternoon were about to change. After all, her desire for her husband had only heightened with the pregnancy. It was little surprise with how well the man balanced her out. He was her complete opposite and perfect compliment.

~

"You are sure you do not want to lay on my arm?" Daniel gave her a teasing grin as he settled into bed and held his arm out.

"Nay." Keturah chuckled.

For three nights, Daniel had used the plight of being injured to attempt to entice her into sleeping in his embrace. Each time they had tried to sleep in such a position, though, she'd laid awake for hours. Until Daniel finally rolled over.

She did, however, take his hand and curl up next to him, her other hand resting on her middle. A smile stretched her face.

Daniel brushed a kiss over her forehead. "Good night," he whispered huskily.

A still tranquility fell over the dark cabin, and Keturah poured her silent thanks out to the good Lord above.

Suddenly, a cry pierced the night. Keturah's grip tightened on Daniel's hand as her eyes popped open. "What was that?"

She closed her eyes and cocked her head to better listen. The cry came again. An eerie, garbling cry that stood the hairs on the back of her neck. Almost that of a woman, but different, louder. In a way, it reminded her of the strange yips of the coyotes when they hunted. But they did so in packs, and this was a single voice. Plus, this was...rougher.

Every so often, the sound repeated, drawing closer. "A cougar." Keturah finally identified it. "But normally, they only mate in the winter."

Daniel climbed from bed and begun pulling his breeches back on. She slipped from the covers as well. As she wrapped a shawl around her shoulders, he went for the rifle over the hearth.

Keturah stopped him with a hand to his arm. "What are ye to do?"

"Scare it away." Daniel's voice was firm, and it was evident he felt the need to protect his family.

"Nay. A cougar is dangerous. It will go on its way."

"What about the horse and cow?"

In this mild weather, the two stayed in the corral even overnight. Keturah frowned. If the large cat was looking to mate, she was not likely concerned with hunting. But could they take that risk?

A squeal sounded outside. Cinnamon.

Keturah whirled around as Daniel stalked out onto the porch and down the front steps. *Please, Lord, protect him.* She rushed toward the door and peered out into the black of night. Daniel raised the gun in the air and shot. Twice more, he reloaded and shot.

Off to their right, a blur moved away, into the night, and Keturah's mouth dropped open. The cougar had been right there, on their homestead. And Daniel had shown not a moment's hesitation in protecting their growing family.

As he stepped back up onto the porch, she went to him and wrapped her arms around his middle, pressing into him and his strength. How could she ever have been skeptical of this man who had only his family's best interest at heart? She needed to stop doubting, stop relying so much on her own strength, and lean into both him and the Lord. With God's help, that's what she would do from now on.

# CHAPTER 12

*September 8, 1782*

Daniel placed another log atop the stump and swung his ax, relishing the satisfying crack that came as metal collided with wood and the log split apart. His arms ached, and his shirt was wet with perspiration, but it was beyond fulfilling to provide for one's family.

Family. The thought brought a smile to his face as he placed another log atop the stump. He could not wait for the day they became a family, when he and Keturah would be joined in this world by their little one. He brought the ax down again as he tried to imagine the baby. Would it be a little boy with dark hair and eyes or a baby girl with locks the color of warm flames and eyes the color of spring? Or maybe the babe would resemble both him and Keturah? No matter what, the child would feel the love he never had. This child would be cherished by both his parents.

A frisson of fear cut through Daniel's heart. What if childbirth claimed his wife as it had his mother? The question had plagued him since Keturah had shared her joyous news. But as he always did when the fear crept in, he whispered a prayer to the Lord that He would bring her safely through delivery.

Daniel lifted his gaze to where Keturah was placing clothes on the line after doing the washing. Yet did not see her. His brow lowered, but his wife was quite capable of caring for herself. She'd likely stopped for a quick rest or a drink of water. He resumed his chopping, lifting another log and splitting it.

A wail stopped him mid-swing and stole the breath from his lungs. His eyes snapped to where more cries came from the outhouse, and his heart plummeted. After dropping the ax, he ran for his wife. Something was terribly wrong.

~

If it were not for Daniel's strong arm around her waist, Keturah would not have been able to stand. But he half ushered her and half carried her as her feet failed to cooperate. Her entire body was numb, and she moved in a daze. Somehow, they made it through the doorway and to the bed. Thankful for the dim lighting of the cabin, Keturah curled into the fetal position and squeezed her eyes shut, as though she could shut out the pain.

But there was no denying the truth. Their baby was gone. The sight of the blood flashed in her mind again, and she clapped a hand over her mouth to hold in a wail. It had taken some time of Daniel holding her and comforting her to stop the cries to begin with. Her heart had been ripped into a million pieces.

Daniel laid the quilt over her, and she gripped tightly to the edge, pulling it up under her chin. Keturah squeezed her eyes tighter still and balled herself further. She could do nothing else. She was trapped within her circumstances. From this moment, she could only wait for the nightmare to pass. Only, it never would. She would never be able to forget that terrible moment in the outhouse. And never would the pain of losing her child end. Keturah nestled into the pillow, numbness consuming her with a ferocity she had never known.

How could this be God's plan?

~

*September 11, 1782*

The gentle weight of Daniel's hand came to rest on Keturah's shoulder, but she did not open her eyes. "Keturah." His soft voice beckoned her to wake. But she did not wish to. She held no desire to reenter the world of the living. Or to partake of the strange-smelling soup that he offered. "Keturah, my love, you need to eat."

Nay, she did not need to eat. She did not need anything except for the one thing that had been taken from her. And there was nothing that could bring it back. Not even the Lord. The Lord had abandoned her. He must have. How could He allow this to happen when He was all powerful? Tears leaked from her eyes again as she squeezed her lashes shut tighter.

"Oh, darling." Daniel set the bowl beside the bed before he swept her up into his arms to rock her while she cried into his chest.

The man had proved himself to be just this side of sainthood over the past few days. In fact, she knew not how many days had passed. Daniel had been a constant companion, continually attempting to care for her, pressing her to keep on living. But Keturah could not bring herself to leave the bed, much less return the love that he so generously gave. All she wanted to do was sleep. For that was the only time she did not have to face the agony.

But as with every time Daniel came to check on her or offer her sustenance, she was awake now. And the pain ripped through her afresh. The heart-wrenching reminder that it was only the two of them. That their bairn would never arrive and make them a family of three. Despite all she had been through...this...this was something she simply could not bear. So the tears flowed unchecked down her cheeks, and her body shook with her sobs as she cried into her husband's sturdy chest. His shirt would soon be soaked, but she could not bring herself to care. She could only pray that the sweet oblivion of sleep would claim her soon.

S*EPTEMBER 19, 1782*

Daniel turned and peered into the black night outside their cabin one more time before he shut the door behind him and put the bar down. On this moonless night, the world seemed to reflect the hopelessness that filled both his own soul and the cabin. He glanced toward the bed where Keturah slept. And though his stomach grumbled, he wondered if he should even prepare anything for supper. What good would it do? Keturah would not eat, and frankly, he did not feel like going through the motions.

He moved into the rocker beside the hearth and settled in with Scamper stretched out on the floor beside him. Daniel opened his Bible and attempted to read, but the words seemed to blur before his eyes. These days, as he walked through the world in a haze with his wife bed-ridden, it seemed the Lord was far away. The old hopelessness that gripped him some nights on the trail, when he had not even Nanny to provide comfort and care, had returned.

He was all alone.

There was not a person in the world to love and care for him in his time of need. Whatever affection had grown between him and his wife seemed to be shattered. For her grief was so strong, she was incapable of returning his love. Daniel could not blame her, not in the least. But it did not leave him any less lonely.

How was it possible, when their baby had been loved and longed for, that it had been taken? He tried to remind himself that the Lord had a plan. In these dark days, it did not seem quite possible, though. He closed his eyes in an effort to pray, but no words came to mind. Finally, he settled on whispering the same prayer for Keturah that he had prayed a million times. *Lord, please ease her grief and help her to know that she is not alone.*

The words seemed to bounce off the ceiling.

*October 16, 1782*

Scamper whined and glanced in the direction of the bed, then up at Daniel. The dog's big brown eyes begged him to explain why his other person was in bed in the middle of the day, instead of outside working where he could run and play.

Daniel frowned down at Scamper as he ruffled his ears. A quiet "I know, buddy," was all he could manage.

Because in his heart, he was as lost as the canine.

More than a month had passed since the loss of their child and still, Keturah did little more than eat and sleep. And she barely ate enough to survive. Daniel loathed to see how her bones had become so prevalent in such a short period of time. His heart ached with not only his own loss, but more importantly, the desire to ease his wife's pain. He could not stand to see her this way, all the fire gone. For once, he longed for the disagreements of old. Sure, his wife was stubborn and spirited. And she sometimes drove him up the wall. But how he wished to see that passion again.

Settling his Bible in his lap, Daniel watched her sleeping form. Well, her still form, at least. Oftentimes, he was not sure if she actually slept or if she just laid there, as numb and hopeless as he felt deep within. What could he do to bring a smile to her face?

His mind drifted to the cinnamon rolls Nanny had made when he was a youngster. Their delectable warmth had always seemed to make the day better, no matter how his family had treated him. He had not the slightest idea how to make them, but he could certainly try.

He quickly rose from the rocking chair and moved to where Keturah normally prepared such food items at the end of the long dining table. Daniel had watched her make biscuit dough countless times. Surely, he could start with that. Glancing around, he pulled out what he thought she normally used and pressed his lips together as he started mixing.

As Daniel plunged his hands into the gooey mixture, he cast a halfhearted smile in the dog's direction. "Here we go, buddy. Let us see what we can do for our girl."

Had their child been a girl? His heart wrenched at the thought. They would never know this side of heaven. Frowning, Daniel worked his hands deeper into the mixture, as though he could work out some of his frustration in kneading the dough.

Just when he and Keturah had seemed to find their footing within their marriage, they were faced with this most terrible heartbreak. Was their union strong enough to withstand this? Or was he destined to watch his wife waste away in bed?

A knot formed in Daniel's throat. Their home had become as cold and empty as his had been growing up. Keturah remained silent even when he convinced her to eat, and she faced away from him each night. He knew her distance was only due to her grief, but it did not make it any easier to bear.

But Daniel would not stand by while she pushed him away, as his father had done to him. He would do all he could to ease her pain. God had brought them together for a reason. While Daniel had failed time after time in life, he could not fail now. Not when his wife needed him the most. He would do all he could to put a smile on her face. Even if that meant making a fool of himself by attempting baking.

After mixing the dough, Daniel retrieved his tin of

cinnamon and attempted to mold the rolls into shape. He grimaced as he surveyed the sticky mess that looked nothing like the delicious treat he remembered. But with any luck, they would still taste as good. He shrugged as he cast a glance down at Scamper, where he laid patiently at Daniel's feet, before he moved to stoke the fire. Then he hung the pot over the flames and set about cleaning up.

By the time Daniel had finished with the dishes, the fragrant scent of cinnamon had begun to fill the room. He closed his eyes and let out a sigh. Maybe the rolls would turn out, after all. Hope stirring within, he lifted the washbasin and took the dirty water out to dump behind the cabin. The crisp autumn air nipped at his nose and sent a chill up his arm where he had rolled his sleeves. Daniel smiled. Life on the Kentucky frontier had certainly changed him. But all for the better.

He had only just dumped the water and turned back toward the cabin when Scamper started barking inside. Daniel's brows drew together, and he picked up his pace. He leapt onto the porch and hurried through the door.

His gaze immediately landed on Scamper, where he stood near the hearth. The dog barked furiously at something beyond the rocking chair. Had a snake or some other varmint made it into the cabin? Daniel moved closer with slow, deliberate steps. When he could see beyond the chair, his heart dropped. As the fire burned, a log had rolled from the hearth.

Keturah's sewing basket had toppled over, its contents strewn between the rocker and the wall, and the smoldering log lay within the fray. The cloth beside it had already ignited, the perfect fodder for the hungry embers.

The dishwater having already been disposed of, he turned for the only other water he knew to be present in their home—the basin beside the bed. Daniel darted across the room, lifted the porcelain bowl from its perch, and returned. Already, the small flames licked at the wall. But he poured the water atop its fiery orange and gold fingers, effectively dousing them before any serious damage could be done. A little soot and a few ruined pieces of fabric were the only evidence that remained of the fire.

With a sigh of relief, he turned to ensure that Keturah had slept through the ordeal. But she had not.

∼

Sitting on the edge of the bed, Keturah opened her mouth, but no words came out as she took in the scene before her. Scamper watched from near the hearth while Daniel stood behind the rocker, her water basin in hand. The contents of her sewing basket were strewn across the floor in a burnt, watery mess, and black soot marred the back wall.

Keturah's eyes flew to Daniel's. "What happened?"

Sliding from bed, she moved closer, her gaze darting from her husband's face to the mess and back.

Daniel's jaw worked before he spoke. "A log must have rolled from the fire and knocked your sewing basket over while I was out dumping wash water." Daniel motioned to a charred lump near her basket. "A small fire had caught, but I put it out."

Fire? Keturah swallowed. They could have lost the cabin, all they had worked so hard to keep. What would they have done then? With no bairn and no home? Tears filled her vision, and she began to shake. "The whole house could have burnt down!"

Daniel's mouth pressed into a line. "I know. Perhaps I should have checked the fire before I went out, but I was only trying to make you cinnamon rolls." At that, his eyes widened, and he ran to the table and retrieved a towel. Then he went to the hearth and lifted a pot from where it hung over the fire. The scent of cinnamon registered, mixed with that of burnt cloth. Keturah fought the urge to wretch.

So this was Daniel's fault. Had she not shown him how to properly stack the logs and tend the fire to prevent mishaps? Her fists clenched at her sides. "Why could ye not leave well enough alone? Ye cannae cook. Ye cannae bake. Stop tryin'. Stop makin' a mess of things." Keturah raged at Daniel. All the pain and grief that had been bottled up over the past weeks finally rose to the surface. And she aimed it at the man standing before her. "I dinnae need cinnamon rolls. I need our home, safe an' sound. And..." A sob stuck in her throat, and she turned away. She closed her eyes tight against the tears. "I need our bairn."

Keturah dropped to her knees and covered her face as she cried. Tears that had remained within for over a month now flowed unchecked. Her grief swallowed her, and she became aware of nothing but the all-consuming pain.

## CHAPTER 13

Scamper followed Daniel, barking after him as he stormed out the door. He ignored the animal. He could not think straight and needed space to cool down and get his head right. He needed room to run, room to stretch his legs and get away from the nightmare that had taken over his marriage. He did not know where he was headed, but his feet moved and he followed. Wind whipped at him as he crossed the clearing where their home sat.

Daniel plowed on, into the woods and to the springhouse. There he stopped only a second. It was not far enough. He had to keep moving, to evade the barrage of emotions that threatened to consume him whole. Turning left, he started up the hillside as large fat drops of water started to fall from the sky. The trees provided cover, though, and only an occasional drop landed on his head and shoulders at first. So he charged farther on, Scamper still on his heels.

The rain increased in strength and force, as did the pain within his chest. The pain of losing their child before they had ever seen its precious face, the pain of a life lost before it had even begun. The pain of seeing his wife so distraught while he remained helpless to do anything about it. The pain of having no one. Absolutely no one he could turn to.

"Why, God?" The outraged cry tore from his lips after being confined for far too long, and he stopped and turned his face to the heavens as rain fell down upon him.

For over a month, he had held in his hurt and anger as he put his wife first. But that had backfired. And now, much as it was for Keturah, the rage could be contained no longer. Daniel kicked a stone near his foot, sending it skittering into the nearby creek. He kicked another and another. Then he lifted a large muddied rock and chucked it as far as he could. A cry tore from his lips as he did so. He latched onto the damp leaves of a fern and tugged. But instead of ripping from the ground, the plant remained firmly in place while Daniel slipped and fell onto his rear. He buried his face in his hands and let the tears fall.

Finally, they came in great waves like the rain that drenched his clothes. His body heaved, and he struggled for breath between sobs. Why did they have to lose their sweet child? What good could possibly come from this? How could this be God's plan?

Daniel cried. He cried for his own loss and his wife's. He cried for the rift that had formed between them. He cried for the deep loneliness that threatened to devour him. How could they ever go on like this? At that moment, Daniel was not sure how he would ever tear himself from that spot of earth and go on living, as though nothing had happened. As if there was not a gaping hole in his heart.

But slowly, his tears slowed, and the unbearable pain within him waned. As thunder boomed overhead, Daniel ran his hand through wet hair and shivered. Scamper pushed a damp nose under his hand and peered up at him with eyes filled with unconditional love and concern. The corner of Daniel's mouth lifted the slightest bit. No matter how alone he felt, he was never truly alone. God had brought him, Scamper, and Keturah together. Though Daniel would never understand why they must be forced to endure such a trial, they were still a family. God had a plan for them, and He would see it through. They need only be faithful.

"Lord, I apologize. I have prayed over and over for You to help my wife, to ease her pain. But I neglected to pray for myself. Please, Lord, help me to come to terms with our loss, to find some way to move forward. Help our family to move forward—together. Help us see the blessings that remain, without focusing solely on what was lost. Help us know You are still with us, even in the midst of our turmoil, and that You will lead us through."

Somehow, God would do just that. He always honored His promises.

Daniel let out a breath as he stood. He needed to take the first step forward and return to his wife. Rain fell harder as he headed toward the cabin, the wind driving it against him. He should have headed back at the first drizzle. Scamper stuck closer to his side as they traversed the soggy earth. Over the sound of rain and between thunder claps, there came another noise. Daniel stopped and gazed down the hill at the creek that fed the springhouse.

Water rolled and tumbled past in what now resembled a river. Daniel swallowed. How would they return home? Should he and Scamper seek shelter until the weather passed? Another shiver passed through Daniel. No, he was soaked through and needed a warm fire before darkness fell. Plus, Keturah would worry.

With a frown, Daniel moved closer. He glanced up and down the visible length of rushing water for a way to cross. Several feet upriver was a large boulder with a tree beside it. The lowest branch appeared to stretch to the other side of the swollen creek. With the strength he had gained from months of manual labor, surely, he could use the branch to cross. From the other side, he could figure a way to help the dog. He went to the tree and climbed up onto the boulder. Daniel jumped up and gripped the branch, the rough bark tearing at his hands.

He attempted to swing his legs up so that he could shimmy down the length of the branch, but his feet missed. His left hand slipped, and a growl rose from his chest as he dug his fingertips into the wood. Below him, Scamper let out a bark.

Daniel changed strategy, swinging his body forward to gain momentum, and he moved his left hand farther along the branch. In this manner, he proceeded along its length, one hand after the other. Halfway across, a crack sounded above the rain, and the branch dipped lower. No. Daniel's eyes widened and his chest heaved. He had to continue on—there was no other way.

He pulled his right hand free and reached forward, but another crack met his ears. The branch jerked, and his fingers found no purchase. Suddenly, he was falling.

~

Daniel gasped before the water claimed him again. It propelled him with extraordinary force, swirling all around him and filling his senses. He fought for the surface, but he could not tell up from down. Something knocked him in the back of the head, and he gasped. His eyes, nose, and throat burned. As did his lungs.

He thought he might drown, but finally, he resurfaced.

Daniel sputtered, then sucked in as large a breath as he could. It was no use, though, without being able to expel the water from his body first. Instead of taking in precious air, he choked and was pulled back under. Daniel fought the current. Was this how he was to die?

No, it could not be. He could not allow Keturah to lose him as well as their unborn child. How could any soul survive that?

~

Keturah paced back and forth in front of the hearth as thunder caused the cabin to shudder. Was this really happening again? Her hands tightened into fists, her nails biting into her palms, as memories of the night her father died flooded back. How the rain had pounded against the cabin in thick, unrelenting sheets before the tornado had come. He had only gone to the barn to ensure all was secure and the animals safe.

But now... she had not the faintest idea where Daniel was. And it seemed history would repeat itself as the storm outside raged with a fury like she had never known. Breathing became difficult, as though air refused to enter her lungs. Keturah's throat burned as she considered the harsh words she had spoken to Daniel. She put her hand to her neck, but there was no relief from the sting that started in her throat and squeezed up, into her eyes. She blinked as tears blurred her vision.

How could she have been so terrible to the man who had shown her only love and grace? While Keturah had wallowed in her own grief, without thought to her husband's pain, he had remained steadfast and caring. Daniel had only been attempting to bring a smile to her face, and she had behaved in a vile manner. Now he was out in the storm. Alone, and possibly lost, because of her.

Letting out a groan, Keturah spun toward the door. She plucked her cloak from its hook and threw open the door to the tempest outside. Her chest constricted. She had to find Daniel, no matter what. After wrapping her cloak around her shoulders, she moved out into the pelting rain, blinking past the water that ran over her face. She glanced around. Which direction would Daniel have gone?

At that moment, Scamper burst through the trees, barking furiously as he rushed toward her. He ran in a wild circle around her before coming to a stop.

"What is it, boy?"

Scamper continued barking, glancing between her and the woods. When she stepped toward him, the dog took off back into the forest. Lifting her skirts, Keturah ran after the animal with blind faith, praying all the while that he was leading her toward Daniel.

Scamper darted in and out between trees,

completely focused on his destination. Keturah sloshed over the sodden earth as she followed. Twigs snapped underfoot as she maneuvered over roots and under a low-hanging branch dripping with water. Mud splattered over her petticoats, and Scamper's white fur had turned mostly brown, but they forged ahead. No amount of mire or muck would stop her from reaching her husband.

*Please, Lord, allow Scamper to lead me to him. An' please let all be well when I find him. Please dinnae let me lose him.*

Tears mixed with the rain flowing over her cheeks, and a lump formed in her throat. Scamper leapt over a downed tree, claimed by the storm, and Keturah scrambled over. "Scamper, wait," she called as she pulled her petticoat free of the rough bark and attempted to catch up with the dog. Clearly impatient, he glanced back and forth as he paused only a moment before continuing on.

Above the storm, Keturah became aware of a faint roar in the background. She stopped and placed a hand on the tall ash tree to her right as her heart began to race. *Please, nay.* Her breaths became ragged as she listened for the sound to grow. But it remained steady.

Scamper barked at her, drawing her attention. Her brows pulled together as she attempted to focus. She forced herself forward, after the dog and past the panic that squeezed her chest. Thunder clapped overhead, and she ducked at the noise. The roar in her ears grew the farther she and the dog went.

Finally, they moved past a towering pine whose needles blew wildly about in the wind, and Keturah's eyes widened as she took in the source of the sound. What had once been a quiet, babbling creek now raged beyond its borders. The muddy waters rolled and churned, with tree branches and other debris captured in its hungry depths. Scamper ventured precariously close to the monstrous beast. She took a step toward him, calling his name, then froze.

Draped over a boulder at the water's edge was her husband, soaked to the bone.

"Daniel," she screamed and dashed forward.

Keturah dropped to her knees in the mud while the water roared past, still tumbling over Daniel's bottom half. Blood, mixed with mud and debris, coated the back of his head, and when she brushed his hair back, his face was disturbingly pale with his lips a deep purple.

*Oh, Lord, please nay. Please dinnae let him be gone from me.*

Tears flowed as she gently placed her shaking hand on the back of his head. Carefully, she attempted to assess the extent of his wounds, but to no avail. She would need to wash away the mess to see properly. But none of that mattered if there was not life within his body.

Hooking her hands under his arms, Keturah pushed against the rock with her foot to slowly pull his waterlogged body from the torrent one slow inch at a time.

Then she rolled him onto his back and leaned close, listening for a breath. No air stirred her cheek. Through the unrelenting rain, she watched his chest with bated breath, but she saw not even the slightest rise and fall.

"Nay. Daniel, ye cannae leave me like this," she cried out.

Keturah shoved hard against his lifeless chest, half in an effort to expel water from his lungs and half out of grief and anger. "Nay," she whispered again as she sat back on her heels and tangled her fingers in her rain-soaked curls.

What was she to do? Daniel was the one person who truly loved her. How could she not have seen that before? How could she have been blind to the fact that all his attempts and failures, all that he had done over the past month, had been for her? He showed her nothing but love and devotion, and how had she repaid him?

Now, because of her selfishness and anger, he had drowned. *Please, Lord. Please bring him back to me.* Sobs tore from her body, and tears streamed down her face.

Suddenly, Daniel began to cough, his chest heaving with his body's effort to rid itself of water.

Keturah scrambled closer, leaning over him once more. "Daniel?"

Her husband rolled onto his side as he spewed water, and Keturah placed her hand against his back, as if she could lend him some of her strength. When he finally ceased coughing, and with some effort, he rose into a sitting position. He propped his arms on his knees as he hung his head and focused on breathing for a moment.

Keturah ran her hand through his dripping hair and earned a lopsided smile in the process.

"I was trying to get back to you," Daniel whispered. His voice was hoarse and raw, and she barely heard him above the din.

Her heart swelled, and her tears changed to ones of joy and relief. She wrapped her arms around him and nestled her head against his. "I know. I know." She nodded as she cried into his shoulder. Despite how cold he was, Keturah was grateful to hold him once more. Never again would she take the presence of her husband for granted.

*Thank Ye, Lord. Thank Ye.*

Scamper yipped suddenly from behind her and bounced around them, reminding them of his company. A broken laugh escaped her as Keturah pulled back and glanced his direction. "Scamper...led me...to ye." Her words came out between the laughter and tears.

"Good boy." Daniel scrubbed the dog's wet ears.

Scamper tilted his head. His tongue hung out as he opened his mouth in what looked strangely close to a smile.

As the rain slackened, Keturah glanced from Scamper to Daniel. Then she gave her husband another hug. Though they may not have been blessed with a child yet, they still had a family. Her, Daniel, and Scamper. And the good Lord above had not left them once. He had been there all along, guiding her and reuniting her with Daniel. Answering her prayers, right from the start. Before He ever brought Keturah and Daniel together, He had been working in their lives. How could she not have seen the extent of His hand in her marriage all these months? And though she may never know why He saw fit to call their baby home, she could be grateful on this day. Grateful for all He had done.

Daniel ran a thumb along her jaw. "Should we head home?"

Keturah smiled up at her husband. "Aye. Aye, we should." Home, with its blackened wall and all, suddenly seemed like the grandest place on earth. And she needed to check her husband's wound. She touched the back of his head.

As her hand lightly rested on a sticky patch of matted hair, Daniel winced. "I am fine," he reassured her. But his voice sounded tired.

"We still need to get ye home an' cleaned up." Keturah forced a smile and stood before reaching a hand down to help Daniel to his feet.

With another grimace, he slowly rose. He wavered for a moment, then wrapped his arm around her shoulders and, without her providing direction, turned toward home.

A small smile stretched Keturah's lips as she nestled

in, slipping her own arm around his middle, before they started the trek home. Limping and slowly, they covered the distance...together.

~

Keturah dabbed a damp cloth at the edge of the wound one last time before she breathed a sigh of relief. The injury was not near as bad as she had feared, maybe the same width as a walnut. She moved around in front of Daniel and looked him in the face. "How do ye feel?"

He offered her a weary smile before he reached out and took her hands into his and squeezed. "I am well," he reiterated once more.

Keturah ran her thumb over his cheek, the skin beneath her finger now reassuringly warm and dry, rather than wet and frigid. "Well, I have to be sure." She peered into his golden-brown gaze, her insides swirling as her cheeks heated. She wrapped her arms around his neck as Daniel slipped his around her waist. "I love ye."

Daniel's grin broadened as he pulled her into his embrace. "I love you too." His voice was deep and enticing as Keturah settled in his lap and curled into him. Both were in clean, dry clothes, and Scamper snoozed by the fire that warmed the whole of the cabin. The moment could not be much more perfect.

But then Daniel stole a kiss that took her breath away, and she melted into him. Into the love that flowed between them and the sweet comfort of his body close to hers. Into the overwhelming joy of being back in the arms of the person she loved, the person God had made for her. And for the first time since the miscarriage, Keturah could not wait to see where God took them from there and how He blessed their future. She would be grateful for every single moment.

~

*November 1, 1782*

The pleasant sound of his wife humming drifted to his ears, as well as the pop and sizzle of bacon in the skillet, the aroma filling the room. Daniel rolled over and smiled at Keturah as she swished about the room. He had no desire to ever go through such a harrowing experience again, but between his near-death experience and a much-needed visit with Margaret the week before, his wife had turned a corner. Finally, even as cooler weather encroached on them, joy filled the cabin. Joy and love.

Daniel slid out of bed and walked over to his wife, catching her by surprise as he wrapped his arms around her.

Keturah gasped before she turned a bright smile upon him and nestled into his embrace.

How could he be so blessed? Not only had God brought him this woman, but He had reunited them when all seemed hopeless. For the first time in his life, contentedness and belonging wove through Daniel's entire being. He was home. And it was the most incredible feeling in the world to know that God had created this home for him. For him and Keturah.

# EPILOGUE

*One Year Later – November 1, 1783*

Daniel had all but worn a rut outside the cabin pacing back and forth along the length of the porch. Iain Donegal glanced his direction but had long since given up on attempting to calm him or his incessant marching. The man lounged casually in the grass while his older son played fetch with Scamper. But there was simply no way Daniel could remain still while his wife was in the cabin giving birth without him. What if something went wrong? What if they lost another child? Or if Keturah died as his mother had? The thought made his chest constrict.

Daniel paused his pacing to turn his face heavenward. *Lord, please see them both through. Please allow us time together as a family.*

When no other words came, he resumed his motion. It did not stop the worry, but it gave him something to do while his wife was in travail. He ached with the knowledge that Keturah was in pain and he could not be by her side. But as soon as Margaret had arrived, she had ushered him out the door. And despite her growing discomfort, Keturah had given him a smile and a nod. What an incredible woman his wife was, capable of much more than he had ever imagined a single person to be capable of.

Over the past year, he had come to learn that she loved just as fiercely as he did. As their souls healed from the loss of their first child, they had come to rest in one another and God, to see them through the trials of life. What a wonderful partnership it had become. One that Daniel thanked the Lord for every day.

Finally, he understood an inkling of what his father must have faced when he lost Daniel's mother. Though it would never justify how he had treated Daniel, compassion welled within him, and a tear formed in his eye. He could not fathom the depth of the pain his father must have felt. How would he continue living if he lost Keturah?

Suddenly, a quiet sound from within the cabin stopped him in his tracks. He turned, cocking his ear to hear it again. When he registered the tiny, mewling cry of a baby, he dashed up to the cabin door.

Before he could open it, it parted just wide enough

for Margaret to hand a small form swaddled in a blanket over to him. "Ye have a healthy baby girl." She gave him a tired grin. "An' yer wife will be ready to see ye in a moment." After blowing a strand of dark hair from her face, she slipped back into the cabin and left Daniel to stare at the closed door. His mouth gaped open with one unvoiced question—did that mean all was truly well?

But his attention was quickly drawn away as the bundle in his arms began to squirm. When Daniel glanced down, the most precious pink face he had ever laid eyes upon captured his heart. And as he caressed the soft skin of his daughter's chubby cheek, wonder replaced every ounce of worry. Dark eyes blinked up at him, and her tongue worked in and out of her mouth.

So lost was Daniel in admiring the new life in his arms that he must have lost all track of time. For it seemed that in only an instant, the cabin door had opened once more and Margaret gestured him inside. Tearing his gaze away from his daughter's face, he moved into the dim light of the cabin and to the bed where Keturah waited for him. Though her face showed her weariness, it reflected the joy he felt within. Before he had even reached her side, she extended a hand to him.

Daniel carefully slid onto the bed and handed Keturah the bundle in his arms. "You are well?" He searched his wife's pale face.

"Verra well." Keturah nodded, love reflected in her bright green eyes as she met his gaze.

"We must think of a name," Daniel whispered as they both soaked in the precious sight of their daughter. So worried they had been that this pregnancy would end in heartbreak as well, they had not allowed themselves to discuss names. As if not naming the child would have made the loss any easier to bear. Still, the past nine months had been spent with bated breath.

"I already know the perfect name." Keturah's voice pushed into his thoughts and pulled him back into the present.

"You do?"

Keturah dipped her chin in a nod, a conspiratorial grin on her face. "Daniella."

The air left Daniel's lungs. It was difficult to squeeze words past the lump that formed in his throat. But he knew what name would go perfectly with his wife's surprise. Their daughter would have a name that showed both the depth of their love for one another and the melding of their two beings, exactly as God had always intended. "Daniella Ceit."

Keturah smiled as tears formed in her eyes. "Perfect." Even as she held their child close, her hand slipped into his.

Daniel looked from her to the miracle in her arms as he squeezed her hand. *Thank You, Lord.*

And those three simple words held more emotion than he could ever voice. Not only had God seen his wife and daughter through pregnancy and delivery, but He had granted Daniel the one thing he had always wondered if he would ever have—a loving family. He would spend the rest of his life thanking the Lord for the woman at his side, the child nestled in her arms, and the love that flowed between them all.

Did you enjoy this book? We hope so!
**Would you take a quick minute to leave a review where you purchased the book?**
It doesn't have to be long. Just a sentence or two telling what you liked about the story!

Receive a FREE ebook and get updates when new Wild Heart books release: https://wildheartbooks.org/newsletter

# AUTHOR'S NOTE

Thank you for joining me for this third installment of the Frontier Hearts series. I pray that you enjoyed Daniel and Keturah's story and their hardships were not too difficult to read.

Unfortunately, their heartbreak in losing their child is one that so many women have had to face. I, myself, experienced a threatened miscarriage during my most recent pregnancy. In that moment in which I was sure that we had lost our child, I received a glimpse into the hopelessness and heart-wrenching grief that these women have to face.

If you are someone who has experienced a miscarriage, I want you to know that I have a deep respect for your strength and ability to carry on. And I pray that you know that you are not alone. May God comfort you and keep you.

Now, on to a lighter note...James Skaggs's Station

## AUTHOR'S NOTE

was a real fortified settlement in Green County, Kentucky. And though fictionalized for this story, James Skaggs and his wife, Mary, were both real people. Unfortunately, the station no longer stands today.

If you enjoyed this book and wish to learn more about my writing, please join my Facebook reader's group, The Reader's Nest, where all lovers of Christ-centered historical romance can find a home.

# ABOUT THE AUTHOR

Andrea Byrd is a Christian wife and mom located in rural Kentucky, who loves to spend time with her family in the great outdoors, one with nature. Often described as having been born outside her time, she has a deep affinity for an old-fashioned, natural lifestyle.

With a degree in Equine Health & Rehabilitation gathering dust and a full-time job tethering her to a desk eight hours a day, Andrea decided it was time to show both herself and her children that it is truly possible to make your dreams come true. Now with over 1,000 contemporary Christian romance novellas sold, Andrea is pursuing her passion of writing faith-filled romance woven with a thread of true history.

## Want more?

If you love historical romance, check out the other Wild Heart books!

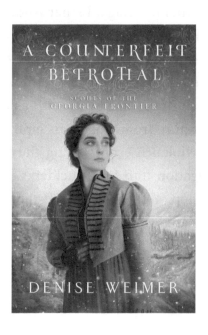

*A Counterfeit Betrothal by Denise Weimer*

**A frontier scout, a healing widow, and a desperate fight for peace.**

At the farthest Georgia outpost this side of hostile Creek Territory in 1813, Jared Lockridge serves his country as a scout to redeem his father's botched heritage. If he can help secure peace against Indians allied to the British, he can bring his betrothed to the home he's building and open his cabinetry shop. Then he comes across a burning cabin and a traumatized woman just widowed by a fatal shot.

Freed from a cruel marriage, Esther Andrews agrees to winter at the Lockridge homestead to help Jared's pregnant sister-in-law. Lame in one foot, Esther has always known she is secondhand goods, but the gentle carpenter-turned-scout draws her heart with as much skill as he creates furniture from wood. His family's love offers hope even as violence erupts along the frontier—and Jared's investigation into local incidents brings danger to their doorstep. Yet how could Esther ever hope a loyal man like Jared would choose her over a fine lady?

∼

*The Road Home by Winnie Griggs*

Unable to operate since a devastating accident, surgeon Wyatt Murdoch is left wondering what to do with his life. He reluctantly agrees to escort two young orphans to their only remaining relative, a great-uncle who lives in Texas. Adventurous Anisha Hayes dreams of belonging. When she comes across a man struggling to control his young charges, she offers her help. He refuses—he doesn't need any help!—but Anisha knows better. Just as she knows the pain of being foisted on unwilling family… How can she convince Wyatt that she has a better option—for all of them?

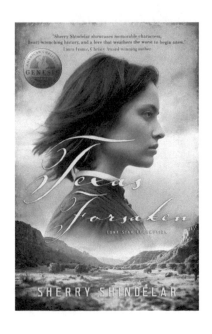

*Texas Forsaken by Sherry Shindelar*
**The man who destroyed her life may be the only one who can save it.**

Seven years ago, Maggie Logan (Eyes-Like-Sky) lost everything she knew when a raid on a wagon train tore her from her family. As the memories of her past faded to nothing more than vague shadows, Maggie adapted, marrying a Comanche warrior, having a baby, and rebuilding her life. But in one terrible battle, the U.S. Cavalry destroys that life and she is taken captive again, this time by those who call themselves her people. Forced into a world she wants nothing to do with, Eyes-Like-Sky's only hope at protecting her child may be an engagement to the man who killed her husband.

Enrolled in West Point to escape his overbearing father, Captain Garret Ramsey finds himself assigned to the Texas frontier, witnessing the brutal Indian War in which both sides commit atrocities. Plagued by guilt for his own role, Garret seeks redemption by taking responsibility for the woman he widowed and her baby. Though he is determined to do whatever it takes to protect them, is he willing to risk everything for a woman whose heart is buried in a grave?

Made in United States
Troutdale, OR
04/05/2024